It was all an incredible dream, of course. The deep voice would fade. . . the warm arms that lifted her head would melt away. . . and the face that went with it would vanish. And she would forget it all. . .

Well, almost all. Not the kiss. Its memory she would cling to, bringing it with her when she emerged from the dream. Because she had never been kissed like that before.

"Stay. . .*stay*. . ." she begged.

His answer was an amazingly gentle kiss. But it still had to be a dream. It was impossible that she would be kissing him back!

5

JUNE MASTERS BACHER is a highly gifted author who shares her talents in *Guideposts* and many other magazines. Her delightful stories and poems have become a trademark, including her most recent books, *Love Is A Gentle Stranger*, *Love's Silent Song*, and *Diary Of A Loving Heart*. Now she brings her art to Christian romance novels, combining her story-telling with mysterious twists in the lives of her characters.

With All My Heart

June Masters Bacher

HARVEST HOUSE PUBLISHERS
Eugene, Oregon 97402

Other Rhapsody Romance Books:

WITH ALL MY HEART

Copyright © 1984 Harvest House Publishers
Eugene, Oregon 97402

Library of Congress Catalog Card Number 83-82701
ISBN 0-89081-410-4

Printed in the United States of America.

To My Husband, George,
With All My Heart!

With All My Heart

The woods are lovely, dark and deep,
But I have promises to keep,
And miles to go before I sleep,
And miles to go before I sleep. . . .

—Robert Frost
American Poet Laureate

Chapter 1

Restlessly, Veronica left her father's bedside to stare through the window overlooking the Atlantic. Seeming to sense her mood, the waters roiled with uncertainty as if awaiting some signal. A dull ache filled her heart. In a quarter hour Dr. Gillian would make his morning call, reaffirming what she knew already. Her father would not live through the day.

At the sound of a low moan, Veronica turned from the window and moved quietly to her father's bedside, careful not to disturb him in case he was dreaming. The pain penetrated his sleep now, the doctor said. His face, looking wasted in the shadows cast by the great oak bed, was immobile. She was about to turn back to her vigil at the window when he spoke feebly.

"... Must talk ... stay, dear daughter ... you must take charge ..."

"Should you talk, Father?" Veronica leaned down with concern. Fever had weakened him, robbed him of coherent thought and speech.

9

"Must...tell secret...you do not own Castle Loma..."

"I know, Father. It will be Mother's until her death. Don't talk."

Weakly, her father reached out. She took the thin, blue veined hands in her own. Tears filled her eyes at the memory of the once powerful hands, so feared by those in his employ, shunned by his wife and son, but so loved by Veronica. These were the hands which, clasped in prayer, transferred to her little-girl heart his firm morals and Rock-of-Gibraltar faith in God's love. Their roughness said work was honorable. Their gentleness and tenderness, known by so few, said marriage was forever. These strong hands, like the gentle voice of their owner, had reassured her—on stormy nights when angry breakers threatened the very hill on which Castle Loma stood— that the beaches were wide. These hands had shaped her life.

In an effort to hide the tears, she turned her head aside. "I must go, Father. Dr. Gillian will be here soon and I have to begin the tours."

"Stay!" he gasped. "We must talk...Castle Loma is *his*...your brother's gambling...responsible in part...other mortgaged...owner a thief...a count..."

Count? The word made no sense in Florida. Noblemen belonged in Europe in suits of armor engaging in sunrise duels, she thought foolishly. Dr. Gillian had warned that at this stage her father might suffer hallucinations. This was a fever-induced dream.

Her father stirred. His voice, when he spoke, was weaker, but his grasp on her hands remained firm.

"You *must* stay...stay and fight...it would kill your mother to leave Castle Loma. Promise me...*promise*..." His voice trailed away.

Fear clutched Veronica's heart. It couldn't be true, of course. Castle Loma had been in the family for three generations, its furnishings and exhibits growing as collector's items from around the world arrived and were put on display. True, the family fortune of her Grandfather Rosemead's generation had dwindled to nothingness. She and Gilbert had never lived the life of the idle rich, but they had not wanted, either. It was only since her father's terminal illness, her mother's accident—which some said was no accident at all—and...well, yes, her brother's gambling debts...that they had decided to open the great house for tours. She had known that there was little cash, but the collections were worth a fortune and the property itself was invaluable. Oh, this was all a mistake! A mistake she must correct so her father could rest.

"There's no problem, Father. Please believe me..."

His mouth twisted in agony. "Promise...you will not let him take this house...from my darling Eleanore... Promise me, Daughter!"

"I promise, Father. I will do whatever you wish to keep this—this count—"

"Count Holman Devonshire...bad blood...black genes...but I have your promise...bring the others...must say good-bye."

That Hugh Rosemead was dying there could be no doubt. Neither could Veronica doubt any longer that his mind was clear nor his words true. What she did doubt was her ability to deal with the shattering news. An unknown stranger of bad blood, a danger, and a threat, was going to take over Castle Loma, the only home she had ever known. Worse, there was no avenue of escape. She was bound by a promise to her beloved father to remain...*but how?* Oh, how could she break the news to Mother? And, above all else, how could she herself cope with her grief? Her father had been her strength.

As she hurried down the long dark hall toward the stairway leading to her mother's bedroom, the subdued voice of the housekeeper told her that Dr. Gillian had arrived.

"Miss Veronica's with him, sir," Hilda whispered.

"Good," the doctor answered, handing her his hat. "I must speak with her."

Veronica paused uncertainly. Then she walked back down the hall to extend her hand to her father's contemporary and one of the few true friends his sometimes harsh and often judgmental nature allowed. Dr. Gillian would be one of the few who would mourn Hugh Rosemead's death with her other than Hilda Elkin and her faithful husband, James.

"Veronica, you are aware—"

"That my father is dying, yes." The words were steady, but her white-knuckled grip on the elderly man's hand betrayed her grief. "He's waiting for Mother and—for you."

The doctor inhaled deeply but made no effort to move. "Does he wish to see your brother also?"

"Yes." And, since there were no secrets between them, Veronica continued, "But Gil is not here. He may be away or—"

"At the Sea Oats?"

"Yes," she said sadly, "he may be at the tavern."

With an impatient wave of his hand, the doctor said, "That whippersnapper should be here."

Veronica nodded. "But he's young, Mother keeps saying—only 22—"

"Two years younger than you," he said bluntly, "and totally responsible for this mess."

Veronica's head shot up. "You know?" she whispered. "Then, it *is* true—all of it?"

"Maybe even more than you know. Hugh did not want to worry your mother. Strange, since the truth of the matter is that she was as involved—but this is not the time. Do not hesitate to call on me later. And now, my child, I must go to your father."

And she must go for her mother. *Help me find the words, Lord,* she whispered, as she moved soundlessly up the carpeted flight of stairs. Halfway up she stopped. Here, where the stairway turned, there was a multi-windowed landing which panned the formal gardens and allowed a view of the main wing of the great house itself.

It was a beautiful castle. It was an ugly castle. Depending on what vantage point of the imagination one viewed it and at what season of the year.

Actually, it was not a castle at all, but rather a many-turreted structure—a mansion in its day—which stood imposingly high on a hill overlooking the marshlands below. On days like today, when the towers were lost in whorls of fog, passersby spoke darkly of the mystery surrounding the great house which had so many guests but so few occupants. Surely, they must be as mysterious as the castle itself. Even the princess-like daughter with Rapunzel hair. . . .

Veronica Rosemead did not think herself mysterious. The fact was that she scarcely thought of herself at all. There was no time. Taking care of Father directed every thought. Mother was not strong enough to help. And Gilbert had no desire. Of course, it was not her brother's fault that he "just didn't have her constitution." Their mother had taken pride that one of her two children inherited her "genteelness." Her overprotectiveness may have helped lead to Gilbert's dependence upon alcohol, his association with questionable companions, and his frequent, unexplained absences. But there was no time for further reflection. With an effort, Veronica turned from the window and walked up the remaining stairs.

Upstairs, there were fewer shadows. Her mother insisted upon light and airiness even though it was in sharp contrast to her dark nature. Today Veronica was grateful for the soft yellows that gave a hint of sunshine to the gloom of the day. Maybe it would make telling Mother easier. Maybe just this once they could talk—

The door to her mother's bedroom was open. Veronica stood in the doorway hesitantly, drinking in the older woman's luminous beauty. Elegant bone structure. Flawless ivory skin. And deeply set, startlingly blue eyes beneath thin, naturally-arched brows. The hair, like Veronica's own, was ripe-cornsilk in color and hopelessly straight and fine, compelling both of them to wear it done in loose upsweeps—not to their liking but adding a classic charm. The strands seemed to be in perpetual motion as if moved about by a breeze nobody felt.

Even as she looked at her mother in admiration, Veronica knew that it was like gazing into a mirror and seeing her own reflection. Physically, they could pass as twins. The sensitive mouths differed only in that Eleanore's lips drew into a straight line of suffering and her eyes, perhaps once brilliant, were dull with life's unpleasantries. Veronica seldom allowed herself to look below the cameo face. The bosom was still youthfully rounded, the arms still unmarred by age—but the rest of her body was immobile beneath the pastel comforters wrapped around the long, useless legs. In the moment she stood there, a pain that must have matched her mother's welled up within her heart. *If only I could have been the one who fell down the stairs,* she thought. And then, *if only I could rush into your arms right now, Mother, and we could share a mutual grief*—

Mrs. Rosemead did not look up. "Why must you stare, Veronica?" she said in irritation. "Why must you be so like your father?"

"I'm sorry," Veronica murmured. "I didn't wish to startle you. I've come for you—"

"Whether or not I wish to go. How like *him* again!"

Wondering exactly how to go on with her mission, Veronica let her mind wander momentarily. It was true.

She was like her father—in all but appearance. She was withdrawn, as Mother said of her so often, leading in the worship services that Hugh Rosemead insisted upon each Sunday morning in the library, but shunning the parties Mother and Gil loved. Her brother, on the other hand, inherited their father's dark handsomeness and their mother's claim to genteelness coupled with undeniable vanity. Veronica had found it strange that each parent chose an unquestionable favorite, based more on the extension of their "spirit" than their "flesh."

Veronica had returned her father's love and generally it was enough. But, at times like this, she wished with all her heart that she and her mother were closer. Maybe then the accident would never have happened. Then, there would be no need for them to remain here....

With a start, she realized that her mind had wandered farther than she had intended. "We must get downstairs, Mother," she said as gently as possible. "The end is close."

To her surprise, Mrs. Rosemead did not object. With a delicate shrug, she allowed herself to be pushed to the electric carrier at the stairway.

Hilda, weeping soundlessly, responded to Veronica's bell and met her mistress at the bottom of the stairs. "Will you send James to find Mr. Gilbert, Hilda?" Veronica called.

The housekeeper nodded. There was no need to tell the woman where Gilbert might be found. Hilda and her husband knew how frequently he was at the Sea Oats and with whom—the rowdier young men of the village and the curvy Rhoda Tucker who served as "hostess" for the tavern and was perhaps more than that to the male customers....

Hugh Rosemead slipped away quietly. Veronica was glad that he was never aware that they were unable to locate his son. He needed no more dishonor than Gilbert had brought to the family name already.

"Do you wish to help us choose a spot in the churchyard, Mrs. Rosemead?" Reverend Crussell asked kindly the following morning.

Eleanore Rosemead, who had shown no emotion during her husband's prolonged illness, burst into hysterical tears, refused to be comforted, and barricaded herself in the upstairs bedroom. Gilbert came home in a drunken stupor and was put to bed by Hilda and James. All arrangements were left to Veronica, giving her no time to think of what lay ahead.

Chapter 2

On one of the few mornings when her brother was relatively sober, Veronica tried to talk with him. "Gilbert," she called softly at his bedroom door. When he grunted sullenly, she opened the door and entered. His eyes were bleary and she was sure his mind was in the same state. But they must talk.

"Gil," Veronica began cautiously, "you know that our resources have dwindled away—" She paused, trying to keep accusation from her voice, then began again, "What can you tell me about the—the incident involving you and Castle Loma? I need the information before we consult with an attorney—"

Gilbert turned bloodshot eyes on her, opening his mouth to speak. His breath reeked of last night's alcohol. His clothes, obviously slept in, were badly mussed. And it was easy to see that he was in a foul mood.

"What're you trying to do, dear sister of mine, protect the family name?"

A sudden anger nipped at Veronica's control. "There's

17

little else to protect," she snapped.

"Go away! You're not welcome in my bedroom—"

His angry words were interrupted by Hilda's soft knock.
"Coffee, Mr. Gilbert?" she asked, opening the door
cautiously ahead of the tea cart.

"You too!" he bellowed then grabbed his head and, with
a moan, fell back into the rumpled bed.

"I could bring him some aspirin, Miss Veronica," the
housekeeper offered.

"You bring me nothing but trouble, the both of you,"
Gilbert's voice was muffled by the covers he had pulled
about his head.

Hilda looked helplessly at Veronica then said quietly,
"Dr. Gillian is downstairs, miss, and there is someone with
him. What shall I tell the doctor?"

"That I will be down shortly. Thank you, Hilda."

When the tea cart rattled down the hall, Veronica turned
back to her brother. She had no idea why her father's
friend wished to see her and certainly his timing was poor
for bringing a guest. Consulting her watch, she saw that
several hours remained before the first tour of the day.
Well, whatever the purpose of the call, she must get as
much information as possible from Gilbert before going
downstairs.

Hoping to muffle the noise of another outburst, Veronica
closed the door. "Gil," she began pleadingly and then
more urgently, "Gilbert! I must have your help. Tell me
something—anything—and we'll see what we can work
out."

"Nothing to tell," her brother mumbled from beneath
the satin coverlet, which was beginning to fray, she noticed. "I'm not to blame that he cheated—or that he took
advantage of my having had a little too much to drink—
probably had them drugged. Now, will you *go*?"

"As soon as you tell me exactly what you signed," she
promised.

"This mausoleum—this tomb of dry bones. No loss if you ask me!" Gilbert's voice trailed off in thick-tongued mumblings.

Veronica's heart sank. Then it was true. All of it. *Not much?* Castle Loma was all the family had—what little there had been left after the mortgage. The *mortgage!* What happened to a mortgage in a case like this? Veronica was no longer heartsick. She was terrified.

"Oh, Gil, Gil," she whispered. "Don't you realize what you've done?"

Her brother's temper seemed to have spent itself. His voice now took on the whine of a spoiled child. "To save my life—or don't you care? I had no choice when he turned the gun on me."

"Gun?" Veronica was stunned. "You mean the man forced you to sign at gun's point?" she asked, grasping at a straw.

"I mean—I signed after—after he'd fired—would have hit me—but for my agility—" His voice trailed off again.

Veronica wanted with all her heart to believe Gilbert. Her brother had his weaknesses, but she loved him. So the man who claimed to own Castle Loma was not only a thief as her father had thought but a murderer as well! A hate foreign to her nature began to take shape.

A subdued murmur of voices downstairs reminded Veronica that she had company waiting. Already Gilbert's snores filled the room so that momentarily her compassion for the boy—*no, he was a man now!*—turned to disgust. Praying that his snores would not be heard below, she made an effort to smooth her silk-fine hair and put her anxieties away. Then, closing the door securely behind her, she descended the stairs, her head held high.

When Veronica raised her eyes at the bottom of the stairs, she was face to face with a man who looked as if he belonged 35 floors above Wall Street in a red-carpeted plate-glass-and-chrome office instead of on the worn

Oriental rug of this time-weathered mansion. His suit was perfectly tailored and in his hand he carried the trademark of an attorney-at-law, an expensive-looking leather briefcase stamped with gold initials, T.S.S. Their gaze locked long enough for her to know that her guest's eyes were very gray, but she was unable to tell if the silvery hair was gray, too, or an unusual shade of platinum.

Dr. Gillian cleared his throat. And Veronica felt herself blush when she realized that not only had she been staring at the stranger but that he had been staring back.

"Good morning, doctor," she said with as much dignity as he could muster, "and Mr.—"

"Shield, Thurman Shield," the man said extending his hand before Dr. Gillian had an opportunity to introduce him. "Attorney-at-law," he added unnecessarily.

The doctor cleared his throat again. "I took the liberty of bringing this young man by as I made some house calls this morning. He's new in the village and seems well versed in Florida laws. I am hoping he can advise you regarding legal matters here."

As he spoke the older man moved into the large reception room, knowing that an invitation was unnecessary. Thurman Shield stepped aside and waved for Veronica to move ahead of himself.

Once seated, Dr. Gillian explained briefly what he knew of the circumstances except for Gilbert's gambling debts and using Castle Loma as a stake. Turning to Veronica, he said, "You can feel free to confide in Mr. Shield, my dear."

"Providing you wish my services," Thurman Shield said politely.

Veronica hesitated. "I don't know," she said uncertainly.

There was understanding in the lawyer's glance. "Of course, you will wish to discuss this with your mother and brother."

"No!" Involuntarily, the word slipped from Veronica's lips. Certainly, she had no desire to alarm her mother until she could get to the bottom of the story and that depended on how cooperative Gilbert was willing to be. But there was such an urgent need inside to talk with someone that before she realized it, Veronica was telling Thurman Shield the entire story.

He listened intently, seeming to read between the lines of anything she may have left out, and then asked for whatever papers she had on hand regarding the mortgage, her father's will, and insurances. Forgetting her concern about his fee, she answered truthfully.

"I am afraid there was little insurance," she admitted. "But, yes, I have a copy of the will in which he names me executrix—and about which I know little." Then, excusing herself, she went in search of the other papers. The visit ended when she located them.

Mr. Shield shook hands with her warmly. Veronica was uncertain how much, if any, he could help the family. But she felt that she could trust the man and that she had found a friend.

The elderly doctor lingered momentarily after the younger man walked briskly toward a well-preserved older-model car. "Nice man," he observed, then added slowly, "I'm not sure just what solution he can come up with, but if worst comes to worst—and you don't mind an old man's opinion—"

"Oh, please say anything you wish," she encouraged.

"Well, as close as your father and I were, I must say that he was highly opinionated—almost fanatical at times. What I'm trying to say is let's not deal too harshly with this Count What's-His-Name until we know the whole story."

Veronica's chin shot up and, resentful of any criticism of her father, she answered coldly, "There is no way we can defend what the man did to us. He has to be a villain!

And I intend to keep my promise to my father. I will do
whatever is necessary to keep this house."

The doctor, who had brought her and her brother into
the world, gave her a little smile of understanding. Then,
picking up his battered black bag, he said affectionately,
"How like Hugh you are—your father's daughter all
right."

A little ashamed, Veronica stood on tiptoe to kiss his
weathered cheek. "I'm afraid I sounded ungrateful. I
praise the Lord for friends like you."

Her eyes misted with tender memories of their
togetherness in her growing-up years. And she noticed that
his hands, as he fumbled for the doorknob, were less certain than they used to be. No doubt there were tears in
the faded eyes of her father's friend, too.

• • •

When Thurman Shield called at Castle Loma several
days later, the news he brought was less than encourag-
ing. "To be blunt, I'm afraid that your father was of sound
mind, Miss Rosemead, when he said that Castle Loma and
all within it are legally the property of one Count Holman
Devonshire. Unfair, indisputably—and regrettable, but the
signed agreement will stand up in court."

"But the gun—wasn't that attempted murder? And his
forcing Gilbert to sign?"

Thurman Shield shook his head. "It would be hard to
prove intent. Witnesses say the shot was fired in self-
defense—that the man's aim is perfect and he could have
killed your brother had he wished." He inhaled deeply
then continued, "The only person who would make an
attempt to defend Gilbert is, at best, a poor one to put on
the stand. A Rhoda Tucker who—er, put him to bed afterward in her bedroom—you understand?"

Yes, she understood. *Too* well. But instead of pursuing the subject, Veronica turned hopefully to another subject. "This count, what were you able to find out about him? That he's a scoundrel, a thief—" She paused when a flicker of a smile crossed the lawyer's face.

"Hardly that, although he may be. But the law deals with facts alone. It is well known that the man is a gambler and somewhat of an adventurer, enjoying somewhat of a fortune."

"Accumulated by others' *mis*fortunes!" she said bitterly. And then, as the full impact of her position penetrated through the grief and bitterness of the past few weeks, Veronica turned to stare helplessly out the window at the restless sea. "Is there nothing I can do?" she half-whispered.

Thurman Shield put on a pair of horn-rimmed glasses, opened his portfolio, and took out a sheaf of documents. While he studied them, Veronica reviewed the situation in her mind, a sense of desolation growing within her. She loved the rambling, castle-like house, although it was her father's presence which made it into a home. It was he who pointed out and named the birds as together she and her father wound slowly up the narrow road to the peak of their privately-named "Enchanted Hill." Each return trip from the village held a sense of adventure... enveloped as they were in a silvery fog of low-hanging clouds drifting in from the Atlantic...then suddenly emerging to catch a first glimpse of the bell tower which Hugh Rosemead, a man of the sea, insisted on equipping with clarion bells and ringing according to "ship's time." Remembering guests who had risen at 4 A.M. when they heard the eight bells, Veronica let a half-smile play at the corners of her mouth.

Suddenly aware of Thurman Shield's eye upon her, Veronica turned with a small gasp. "I—I'm sorry," she murmured trying to remember the question he had asked.

"Don't apologize," he said softly. "I was thinking how very beautiful you are."

Taken by surprise, Veronica felt her cheeks redden. She tried to meet his steady gaze but dropped her eyes in spite of herself and said demurely, "Thank you, Mr. Shield."

"Thurman, please—and may I call you Veronica? It's a fitting name. It has a quaint ring, untouched by the world."

"My father named me," she said, trying to keep her tone matter-of-fact. "And, yes, you may use it."

"Thurman," the lawyer prompted.

"You may use it, Thurman," Veronica said with what she hoped was the right mixture of friendliness and let's-get-back-to-business.

Thurman Shield took his cue. "I wish I had better news, Veronica. It's obvious that you love the place."

Yes, she loved it. . . but it would be impossible to explain that her feelings were more for her mother than for herself. It was her father's wish for Eleanore Blazedale, **regarded by him as his perennial English bride**, to live out her days in the aura of elegance with which he had surrounded her. Mother could never reconcile herself to living like "ordinary people." Secretly, Veronica wondered if her mother had considered her husband and daughter as "commoners." She had not minded the tours of Castle Loma. They had a certain charm. But she had been most distressed with the souvenir shop. It was all right to be "genteelly poor." But *shopkeepers? Ugh!* Unacceptable. . . .

Veronica realized with a start that Thurman was waiting for some sort of response. "Just tell me the bad news," she said.

"There is no money. Debts are enormous. Then, there's the mortgage which will become the responsibility of the new owner. I see no way possible in which you could deal with Holman Devonshire unless you have other resources?"

Veronica shook her head sadly. "But what am I to do about my promise?"

Veronica had not intended to make mention of her father's wishes. They were personal—not something a lawyer could grant at will. But seeing the question on Thurman's face, she told him briefly about Hugh Rosemead's dying request. She could see by his look that the attorney had no solution.

"What are you prepared to do—by way of work?" he asked, obviously looking ahead to her inevitable move, promises or no promises.

"Nothing—nothing at all." Veronica tasted the words for the first time herself. "My father saw to it that my brother and I had fine liberal arts educations and surrounded us with beauty. But," she ended with a catch in her voice, "somehow none of us looked ahead, I guess."

"There would have been no way to anticipate your brother's folly, Veronica. Please don't be offended—"

When he paused, Veronica shifted the subject. "I don't know how to thank you, Thurman. If you will name your fee—"

The young man lifted his hand in protest. "I can accept no fee. So far I have not set up an office and it was a pleasure to have something—and someone as charming—to absorb my time. Besides," he added, wiping his glasses and returning them to their case, "I do not wish to be dismissed, I am hoping that we will be able to see one another—that you will not be leaving—"

"I don't know what we will do," she said truthfully. "My mother knows nothing of our predicament yet . . ." She shuddered visibly at the dread of breaking the news, **then regaining a measure of control, added,** "But you are welcome to come. Every day is open house here—which reminds me that it is time for another of our tours."

Thurman Shield ran a long-fingered hand through his silver-toned hair. "When do you expect the new owner?"

The question caught Veronica off guard. To talk of the matter in businesslike tones was one thing. To pin down a time of arrival made it real. The impossible situation was no longer a poorly-plotted melodrama in some late-late show. The new owner would be coming to evict the three of them. Oh, whatever were they to do?

Shaking her head in despair, Veronica said in a small voice, "Do you believe in prayer?"

"But of course!"

"Then pray for me," she said.

"I have already done that," he answered taking her hand briefly and then hurrying away.

She watched him stride away, a tall, somehow lonely-looking figure who looked strangely out of place in the formal gardens surrounding Castle Loma. When James Elkin, the gardener, raised his head from rose-pruning to wave, Veronica saw Thurman Shield smile for the first time. He was younger and more attractive than she had realized. Just who was he anyway? And what was a man of his obvious intelligence and education doing in this small Atlantic village?

There was no more time to ponder the question. Already guests were ascending the crumbling marble steps out of the fog mists and onto the sun-touched terrace. Quickly, Veronica checked her itinerary and found that she had scheduled a tour of the assembly room where Sunday services were held. On the way to greet the guests, she checked to see that the antique hand-carved tables, overstuffed chairs and sofas, and precious art objects her father had collected from all over the world were in place. They were. And Hilda had thoughtfully laid a fire in the French Renaissance fireplace, the conversation piece of the 80-by-40-foot room. Quickly lighting the fire, she hurried out to greet the guests.

When the day drew to a close, Veronica made an effort to persuade Gilbert to accompany her upstairs to discuss the situation confronting the family. Her brother flatly refused, barricading himself in the bathroom. Moments later she heard the revved-up roar of his sports car. Then a grind of gravel told her that he had left—undoubtedly for the Sea Oats. Gathering as much courage as possible, she went to talk with her invalid mother—wishing again with all her heart that they were closer.

Eleanore Rosemead, beautiful in a black velvet robe piped in white satin, became even more agitated at the financial news than Veronica had expected. Her behavior was startling, a far departure from her usual detached, remote manner. With color high in her usually pale, translucent face, she decried her husband's "extravagance" and Veronica's "poor management" of the estate.

"How are your poor brother and I to live? Oh, I might have known something like this would happen! I might as well be dead...if he'd been successful in killing me outright instead of leaving me a helpless cripple!"

"Mother, please try to calm yourself," Veronica begged. "You know Father loved you dearly, that he wasn't capable of—oh, Mother—" On impulse she dropped to her knees beside the wheelchair. "Can't we talk—try and **understand one another?**"

Mrs. Rosemead's weeping stopped. Drawing her lips into the inevitable tight line, she said impatiently, "Get **up, Veronica, and bring Gilbert to me. You,** not I—his wife—were your father's confidante. You have access to his papers—should know how to save this home. Unless," she added, her once-beautiful blue eyes cold with anger, "you wish to put an end to my suffering—finish the job your clumsy father started!"

Veronica rose obediently, her heart bleeding with remorse at her mother's rejection. It would be easy to hate the spiteful, helpless, self-pitying woman. There was no hope of Eleanore's approval, understanding, or even her love. *But she is my mother and I promised my father....*

She resolved anew to find a way to keep Castle Loma as she went to find her brother. And, unwilling to respond to her mother's wrath, Veronica turned her own toward the fortune hunter who preyed on helpless widows and their children. An unscrupulous phony with a counterfeit title...Count Holman Devonshire indeed!

Chapter 3

During the days that followed, a tomb-like silence closed in at Castle Loma. Veronica continued the tours out of financial necessity. Guests, who sometimes seemed as curious about the owners as they were in the priceless collections they paid to see, were her only contact with the outside world. Her mother, never much of a participant anyway, declared the Sunday services "improper during our period of mourning." So the services were discontinued much to Veronica's disappointment. On occasion, she found herself resolving to resume the Sunday-morning worship as soon as possible, only to realize with a sick heart that any Sunday morning could be their last one here. On those times, she would renew her vow to regain Castle Loma whatever the price.

So the gardens became her solace. While several of them were formally-edged paths leading to priceless sculptures of cherubs, gods, and goddesses, Veronica preferred the more inviting garden at the foot of the great retaining wall. The wall, a necessity because of the various levels of the grounds, also served as an ivy-draped background for a profusion of wild and domestic flowers.

One afternoon after the last tour of the day, made particularly difficult by complaining children and rude adults, Veronica walked down to her Secret Garden to be alone and think. The winter had been especially bleak, the weather seeming to align itself with the atmosphere within Castle Loma. But today there was a hint of spring, the feel of growing things. Before sitting down on a bench, Veronica paused to look down at the sea. Today it was placid and blue, the smooth surface broken only by a few sailboats. But she shuddered involuntarily at the recollection of stormy days when the threat of an approaching hurricane turned the waters gray and pitiless, the billows crashing against the safety wall her father had engineered to protect the great house and his family. She had always felt safe here because of the wall and because of her father's presence. But now—now he was gone. Had the wall been checked for safety lately? Oh, there was so much she must think about. . . .

But not now! This precious hour was hers. So thinking, Veronica cleared her mind of all problems and walked down the little footpath, which only she knew, to a nest of crimson tulips. How beautifully God had arranged nature, she thought. The tulips did not mind the smell of wild onions growing right alongside them at all. If only human beings could be so wise!

Below her, the orange tints began to fade from shop windows. Already a little breeze shivered along the spines of the seedling grasses. Veronica sat down, letting the feel of nature caress her skin, its smell penetrate her nostrils. And then her lips moved in silent prayer—asking the Creator nothing at all, just praising Him for life.

How long she sat there, Veronica was uncertain. And certainly she was unaware of her own beauty—a tall, but slight figure, her softly-upswept hair luminous in the light of the setting sun, seated in a maze of flowers—as seen by an outsider. She had come here to be alone. This was her Secret Garden.

But suddenly there was an intruder! Veronica felt rather than saw eyes upon her. And there had been no warning sound of approaching footsteps because of the heavy undergrowth. Opening her eyes, she found that, much to her surprise, she was looking into a man's face, one of the most handsome faces she had ever seen. A slight frown of puzzlement creased his brow, seemingly at discovering her here. She saw, too, that there was a tense look to the crisp, chiseled line of his jaw and the slightly aquiline profile, like a giant bird that was equally at home on land or sea.

For a moment, Veronica thought she must be imagining the presence of the stranger. Impossible, of course, for the eyes—one of them a deep green and the other a dark brown!—were very much alive. And they were fixed upon her in undisguised admiration. A slight smile played at the corners of his mouth.

"*You*, my dear, are staring!" The stranger swept off his hat—*why, nobody wears a hat these days*, she thought foolishly—and he bowed with a flourish. "You must be Miss Rosemead?"

Veronica, aware only of the short, thick crop of russet-brown hair as the man bowed and his rich, deep voice as he spoke, could only nod. What a frump he must think her!

"Then allow me to introduce myself. I am the Count Holman Devonshire, new owner of the Castle Loma."

Ironically, the clouds shifted to block out the sun. Followed by the warning smell of rain. And mint. The intruder had trampled Hilda's prize peppermint.

"You're standing on the mint," Veronica said realizing that the words must sound insane to Holman Devonshire.

She was right. The smile that had begun moments ago

disappeared as quickly as the dying rays of the afternoon sun. "I had expected to be greeted with kindness, not resentment."

"Kindness!" Veronica suddenly found her voice, putting into it all the anger she had stored against the man. "How could you expect kindness from any of us? Of course we resent your presence here—all of us, my mother, my brother, and I!"

"Ah, my dear Miss Rosemead, but that is where you are wrong," he said mockingly. "Your mother and I have had a fine chat and find that we have much in common. I own this house. She wishes to remain in it. And, to be honest with you, neither of us is over-endowed with scruples as to how we accomplish our ends."

How dare her mother attempt to deal with this admittedly unscrupulous man in her absence! *This,* she thought desperately, *may very well be the most disastrous part of the story yet. Already I am at a disadvantage—*

Holman Devonshire interrupted her thoughts with an impatient, "Well, Miss Rosemead? Have you no wish to hear the terms?"

Terms? The two of them had come to some *agreement?*

Veronica rose with as much dignity as possible. "I am not interested in your terms," she said coldly. "My mother is in no condition—"

"Condition? Don't you mean *position?*"

Veronica cringed at the implication of his words. "My mother is an ill woman," she said in a low, bitter voice. "You had no right to take advantage of her, but you are an old hand at that!"

The laugh he gave was sardonic. "I am beginning to think," he said with ill-disguised disappointment in his disarming stare, "that it was she who took advantage of me!"

"I have no idea what you are talking about—"

The man shrugged his shoulders in the gathering

twilight. "Am I to assume that the three of you had not discussed my being here and the offer the grieving widow was going to make?"

Veronica chose to ignore the rude reference to her mother's widowhood. "Of course we were expecting you. But I had hoped to be the one to speak with you about our staying—somehow."

"Oh, come now, let us not be coy. I like it much better when you are clumsy."

"I am not clumsy—get off my mint bed!"

"You are clumsy with words. And I remind you that I own this garden as well as the house and the property it stands on. So I shall stand where I choose. Right now it pleases me to stand in this stinking bed of mint—" The words were interrupted by an explosive sneeze.

Veronica took pleasure in the violent sneeze. She hoped this fortune hunter was allergic to everything on the grounds. Immediately, she regretted the thought. A man who would take advantage of an irresponsible youth obviously under the influence of alcohol and a woman recently widowed would stop short of nothing. Certainly the lives of her father's beloved trees and shrubs would be meaningless also.

"Come, come!" Holman Devonshire spoke again, his English accent slurred slightly by the sneeze. "You spoke of planning to approach the subject yourself. Do *you* wish to propose?"

Veronica was so buried in her wild thinking that she failed to hear a sudden rumble of thunder. She could only stare at this madman, too shocked to speak. *Propose?* Did he mean...oh, he couldn't! She was reading too much into his words. Then what...?

But she had waited too long. Taking her silence as an approval of sorts, it was he who spoke. "Then you accept *my* offer?"

"What offer?" The words, no more than a whisper,

were all but lost by a louder clap of thunder.

"Why, to marry you, of course!" And he might as well have added, *My Stupid One.*

"M-marry you—marry *you*? Are you out of your mind?"

"Would you stop that exasperating way of parroting back every word I say! The answer to a man's offer to enter the honorable state of matrimony is a simple *Yes* or *No.* In your case, I can see little choice—" He sneezed again but regained his composure and resumed almost immediately in a nasal voice, "but to accept a marriage of convenience."

"I have every choice in the world—" she began. And then she stopped short, remembering her promise to Hugh Rosemead. Mother knew nothing of the promise, of course. Mother was interested in her own welfare—hers and Gilbert's. . . .

A tentative raindrop landed on Veronica's hot cheek. A quick look at the churning black sky overhead said the storm clouds could let go of their burden without further warning.

"We must go!" she said and made a quick step to get past Holman Devonshire. But with more speed than she would have believed possible by any man, his long arm shot out and his strong fingers gripped her arm to make her a virtual prisoner.

"I am not accustomed to being ignored. And certainly not in a matter as vital as this!" he hissed.

There was no opportunity to reply. The two of them were enclosed by a drenching curtain of rain.

"Let go of me! Let go!" Veronica cried the words over and over, her voice drowned out by a wind which had whipped in from the sea.

But, mercifully he had come to his senses. The two of them were running side by side up the narrow path leading toward the enormous house which seemed to grow farther and farther away as they pushed against the rain.

Holman Devonshire held tightly to her arm no matter how
she struggled and she was aware that he had managed to
remove his leather jacket with his free arm and somehow
wind it around her shaking shoulders. Hopelessly, her hair
fell from its loose knot and matted against her face, adding to the difficulty of seeing ahead. Several times she
stumbled. Each time, his hands steadied her. But when
the wind gave a sudden, wild blast she crumpled at its
force and fell to her knees. Without hesitation, Holman
Devonshire swung her up into his arms. It would have
been childish to pound against the massive chest. Already
the new owner of Castle Loma thought she was stupid and
clumsy. She would do nothing to add to that image. So,
closing her eyes to avoid the rain, she relaxed against the
warmth of his body.

"You can open your eyes now!" There was a teasing
note to his voice. "The boogeymen have all gone away."

Veronica's eyes flew open and to her embarrassment the
clouds had all but dissipated. The two of them were standing in a circle of light from the lamp by the upper-garden
gate. And she was looking up into the amused eyes that
were so distracting—one green, the other brown, but more
alike than she'd realized when seen at close range because
they were both flecked with gold. What a ridiculous thing
to be thinking about!

"Put me down immediately," she said in a low, angry
voice—wondering which of them she was more angry
with.

The man set her on her feet carefully. "I am accustomed
to asking toll of those who make use of my services," he
said, resuming the mocking tone of voice. "However, I
shall not require that in this case. Your answer will be
quite payment enough."

Before Veronica could tell him that she had the answer
at this very moment, James called in a concerned voice,
"That you, Miss Veronica?"

"Yes, thank you, James," Holman Devonshire answered for her. "The mistress is quite safe with me."

"Thank you, Your Highness."

Your Highness! Then this impossible man had been laying down house rules to the help already. Well, she would put a stop to *that*...and then she realized anew that she was in no position to put an end to *anything* concerning the Castle Loma.

Without another word, she ran toward the door, thankful that he did not see the tears streaming down her cheeks.

Veronica was relieved when the door swung open to admit her, but relief turned to immediate alarm. A grizzle-toned monster of gigantic proportions bounded through the door. The beast had no eyes. Nothing but blue merle shag for a face. The enormous square body coated with heavy, hard hair. And a tail, like the eyes, was missing! All this she noted as the animal charged.

"Help!" she shrieked. "Somebody get this brute—"

"*Brutus!*" Holman Devonshire corrected. "Not *Brute.*"

The dog, an Old English Sheepdog she was to learn later, crouched obediently at his master's feet. "I'm so sorry, Miss Veronica," Hilda, obviously agitated too, pulled Veronica into what she considered safer quarters inside the vestibule.

"You have nothing to fear, Hilda," the dog's owner assured the housekeeper. "Brutus is as gentle as a lamb—when properly handled."

So, she was clumsy again! Veronica did not care a fig for what the man thought . All she wanted was to escape the whole hateful scene. With that thought in mind, she hurried toward the stairs. But her mother's voice called from the sitting room, "I would like to see my daughter, Hilda—at once."

Veronica stopped short. Mother was in the sitting room? But that was the first time she had left the confines of her bedroom since the death of her husband. With concern, Veronica turned back and entered the door to the left wing of the house—noting as she did so that Holman Devonshire and his Brutus had the tact not to follow. Surprisingly, the dog, his great body pressed to his master's left knee, walked obediently alongside in a peculiar shuffling gait.

"Veronica!" Her mother's voice came from a shadowy corner of the room. The drapes, drawn against the storm, had not been opened. "Where have you been and what on earth happened to your hair? We have a guest!"

"The *guest* and I were in the garden. And the storm happened to my hair. If you will excuse me, Mother—"

"I have not dismissed you!" Eleanore Rosemead said sharply. "You will sit down, please."

"I can't sit down, Mother—not in these wet clothes—"

"There's a matter we must discuss. Now!"

Conditioned to control even the slightest suggestion of resentment toward her ailing mother, Veronica pushed away irritation at the older woman now. Tiredly, she said, "Mother, I am wet and cold. This-this count, as he calls himself, has talked with you and he has talked with me. There is no point in your going over it again."

"No point?" Mrs. Rosemead frowned delicately. "What are you saying, Veronica? That you are too selfish to consider such a generous and businesslike arrangement? Did you listen to the count's terms?"

Veronica sneezed unexpectedly. In a hurry to get away, she admitted that she had not asked what Holman Devonshire expected of her in exchange for the right to remain at Castle Loma.

"Then there *is* something for us to talk about!" her mother said triumphantly. And, without waiting for encouragement, she continued, "The count asks for very little. He wants a cultured hostess and, although you have not taken on the genteelness that seems to come naturally with your brother, I believe that with some concentration on your part, you could—"

"Please, Mother—"

"Don't interrupt, Veronica! Maybe the marriage may not be entirely to your liking, but you are too much of a recluse to expect a long line of admirers—called these days, boyfriends I believe. But then, the arrangement may not be the ideal with so eligible a 30-year-old bachelor either—" Here Mrs. Rosemead paused as if uncertain that her daughter was moved by her words and continued pitiously, "but I am at your mercy. Surely you will not see your helpless mother evicted without any more compassion than your father!" A fluttering hand went to the bosom of her hostess gown.

Then Veronica made the mistake of her life. "How can you say Father had no compassion, Mother?" she cried out in his defense. "His dying words were that I promise—"

Immediately, she could have bitten off her tongue. And, as expected, her mother picked up the slip. Eyes alight with renewed interest, she leaned forward. "Yes? What promise did you make that is so secret you cannot discuss it with your own mother?"

"That's not true, Mother. It's just that I have been trying to think it through before worrying you—"

"The *promise*, Veronica!"

"That I would not allow you to be removed from your home," she said in a small, sad voice—wondering if the revelation showed weakness or strength. She knew only that she felt sick, tired, and drained.

Murmuring something that probably made no sense, Veronica fled from the room. Halfway up the stairs, she ran head-on into Holman Devonshire. Clumsy...*clumsy*!

"Get out of those wet clothes!" His words were an order.

"Get out of my way!" Veronica flared back.

Then, to her embarrassment, she sneezed, an act that

made the new owner of Castle Loma spin on his heel as he was descending the stair and look at her with threatening eyes. "Do as you are told or I will carry you bodily into a hot bath."

Veronica turned and raced up the stairs. Slamming and locking the door behind her, she stood trembling in the center of her pale-blue and gold bedroom. So many emotions flooded her being that she was unable to catalog them. Anger. No, *fury!* Fatigue. Heartbreak. Shame. And, overlaying it all, a deep sense of helplessness like a small animal caught in the steel jaws of a trap devised for a far more intelligent and experienced victim. Where could she turn? She knew so few. She ached for her father as never before. . . .

• • •

It was a totally different Veronica Rosemead who descended the wide, polished stairs for dinner two hours later when the bell tower chimed to indicate 8:30. She wore a soft blue blouse with a ripple of becoming ruffles at the neckline and an oyster-white button-down skirt. Her pale silver hair refused to stay up in its usual coil at the top of her head, so Veronica resorted to a soft coil at one ear. Deciding she needed something for balance, she added a gardenia behind the other ear. With head held high, she entered the dining room. It would never have occurred to her to ask to be excused from the dinner table. Her training went far too deep for that. One did not show one's emotions. One carried on.

Holman Devonshire rose gallantly from his chair at the table where he, Eleanore Rosemead, and Gilbert—who had not shown his face for . . . how long was it anyway?—awaited her arrival.

"Lovely," said Holman Devonshire with a strange note of pride in his voice. Veronica winced but could think of no way to defend herself against his possessive manner. His tactics were a constant surprise.

"She does at that," Gilbert agreed, rising lazily from his own chair.

Holding back a sneeze, Veronica murmured a polite "Thank you" and was about to indicate to Hilda that they were ready for the first course when Holman Devonshire rang a tiny silver bell beside his plate. When Hilda appeared, he said, "You may serve now, Hilda."

So the new owner had not come to just view his assets then check into a hotel in the village. Neither had he come as a house guest. He had moved in bag and baggage and, without a "by your leave," taken over management of the household and its occupants. And *politely!*

Holman Devonshire's manners were without flaw. Try as she would, Veronica was unable to snuff out a certain reluctant admiration for this cunning intruder who remained standing until she was seated between her brother and himself. No, there was no flaw...other than the unpardonable arrogance, his unscrupulousness, his total lack of compassion...moral or spiritual values! "A thief," her father had called this man of questionable title who had swindled a family of their birthright and brazenly usurped her father's place at the head of the table as if he belonged there. There was honor among thieves, she had heard. *Some* thieves, maybe. But there wasn't a shred of decency in this one....

Veronica was suddenly aware of the silence around her. In the contrast of the warm room and the chilly garments so recently stripped off, she felt a certain sense of languor. A desire to let reality float away...to believe that all of today's happenings were an incredible dream...that she was seated to the right of a wide-shouldered man with a lean waist, a pair of long limbs, and strong arms—a man who belonged here....

But he *didn't!* With an effort, Veronica pushed aside

the dangerous illusion. Careful. She must be *careful.*
Nothing in her ascetic life had prepared her to deal with
a fortune hunter who had no Christian conscience. Her
father had tried to warn her and here she was, at the first
opportunity, allowing herself to be drawn into his spell,
taken in by his charm like some new-money shopper who
was unable to tell a precious gem from a paste imitation.

In an attempt to calm her emotions, Veronica glanced
into the eyes of the intruder—correction, her *host!* Holman
Devonshire's peculiar eyes glowed with an admiration (she
refused to call it *warmth!)* that brought color to her cheeks.
Angered by her lack of composure, she knew that any
words he was waiting for would falter. Make her his
laugh-object. Label her clumsy.

Well, at least, she could *act!* The compelling eyes were
still locked with hers. A smile that he managed to make
appear sincere curved his handsome mouth. With all the
courage she could muster, Veronica answered that smile
almost coquettishly—letting her candlelit eyes linger on
the obviously surprised face a moment. Not long. Just long
enough to set him back on his heels, she realized with
satisfaction.

And for that moment she had the advantage. But
moments do not last. Holman Devonshire swiftly regained
what territory he had lost.

"I was wondering, Miss Rosemead, if there is a special
custom the family observes around dinner. You do serve
as official hostess?"

"Oh, yes, my daughter *is* our official hostess, Count
Devonshire," Veronica's mother spoke for her. "And quite
a gracious one," she added, making the situation all the
more embarrassing.

Shame flooded Veronica's being. Holman Devonshire was right. Her mother had as few scruples as
he when it came to gaining her own ends. Perhaps
her father should have warned the new owner against

his wife instead of trying to protect her from him.

"I am aware of that, Mrs. Rosemead," Holman Devonshire said with just the right touch of appreciation and reprimand. "Miss Rosemead? Or may I call you Veronica?"

Caught as she was in the presence of an ill mother and a sullen brother, either of whom was capable of making a cruel scene, Veronica had no choice.

"Of course," she said, studying the Haviland china plate before her as if it were new. When there was no further conversation, Veronica realized that she had left the question unanswered. All right! He had asked for it.

"My father always said grace."

Holman's laugh was light—amused, perhaps—but not mocking. "May I confess that I am out of practice and ask you to do the honors? Or," he paused daringly, "is it proper to expect the male member to assume the duties? If you wish to defer to your brother—"

Gilbert? Oh, perish the thought! "I will!" she said too quickly and too enthusiastically, her heart thumping unevenly in her chest.

"As you wish." With Holman Devonshire's words, Eleanore Rosemead and her son bowed their heads along with him.

"Therefore, I will look unto the Lord; I will wait for the God of my salvation; my God will hear me," Veronica began one of her father's favorite passages from the prophet Micah. Her voice, low and uncertain at first, resumed its natural soft, musical tones as she forgot those around her and engaged in the words of praise.

> Rejoice not against me, O mine enemy:
> when I fall I shall arise; when I sit in darkness,
> the Lord shall be a light unto me. I will bear
> the indignation of the Lord, because I have
> sinned against Him, until He pleads my cause,

and executes judgment for me; He will bring
me forth to the light, and I shall behold his
righteousness. *Amen!*

"That was beautiful, Veronica," Holman Devonshire ap-
plauded. "I think we should make this a regular practice."

"It is already," Veronica reminded him curtly.

Mrs. Rosemead tried to catch her daughter's eye and,
failing, cleared her throat delicately. The moment was
saved when Hilda brought in a pewter tureen of cold
avocado soup.

The rest of the dinner hour was without incident.
Veronica would never remember the food set before her
or the small talk that seemed to flow between her mother
and the count. She recalled only her awareness of a sullen,
almost fearful, attitude Gilbert had fallen into and her
mother's embarrassingly obvious efforts to impress
"royalty" with her daughter's merits. After a time she gave
up trying to cope with humiliation and grew sad instead.
Sad because her mother's first compliments to her came
at a point in her life when they no longer had meaning.

Chapter 4

Veronica spent a restless night and awoke with a headache. She almost wished yesterday's sneezes had developed into a cold, giving her an excuse to remain securely behind her bedroom door. Then she realized such thinking was foolish—there were the scheduled tours. It occurred to her as she dressed for the day that she should have discussed the tours with the new owner of Castle Loma. Surely he had more class than to discontinue them without notice...leaving tourists stranded with meaningless tickets...causing more talk than there was around the village—some of which the tourists were aware of, she was sure. He wouldn't—would he? There was no way of telling. He was too unpredictable. Too erratic. Too—

A soft rap on the door interrupted the thought. "Yes?" she called, quickly pushing the last pearl button through the top buttonhole of her floral silk blouse.

"May I have your breakfast tray brought up so we can talk?" Holman Devonshire's voice was velvet-smooth, but the words were an order in spite of the questioning tone.

"No," Veronica said quickly. "I prefer going down for my meal."

"Fine, so do I. Are you dressed?"

"Yes, I will be down soon," she answered through the curtain of her hair as she prepared to sweep it up.

With a quick motion, she swung the hair up and was about to secure the soft chignon when she found herself looking into the burning eyes of Holman Devonshire's reflection in the mirror of her vanity.

"How dare you look into my mirror," she began stupidly, her mouth filled with hairpins. "I mean—how dare you break into my room!"

"The door was ajar, which hardly constitutes breaking and entering—especially in a man's own house." The tone was patronizing and the face looking back at her in the mirror gave no real cause for alarm. But something in his manner frightened Veronica.

Her hands trembled as she tried to secure the hairpins. "All the same I am entitled to some privacy as—as—"

"As a what?" Did she imagine a tone of intimacy?

"A—*a lady*," she sputtered.

"That I would never question."

"And—your guest," she added although the hateful words were like long fingers closing around her throat. "Your unwilling and unwelcome, I am sure, guest—until I can do something—" Her voice betrayed despair in spite of the effort Veronica made to control it.

The figure in the mirror moved toward her. She met his eyes coldly in the glass. "That is the matter I have come to discuss, Veronica. And I must apologize for entering as I did. As big as this house is there seems to be no place for privacy—if indeed one can ever move beyond the prying eyes of your mother." He paused as if waiting for her to challenge the statement and seemed momentarily taken aback when no challenge came. In this matter he was correct. His tone was measured and cool when he continued

in spite of his standing too close—so close that she could
see his nostrils flange with each breath. Uncomfortably,
she looked away, hating herself for it and missing the first
words.

"—but your brother, given to imbibing, seems to have
done so again. Hilda and James were trying to put the chap
to bed undetected." Holman Devonshire shrugged. "I felt
it was best to allow them to play your mother's little
game."

"Thank you for that," Veronica murmured. Then, in an
attempt to put a safe distance between them, she brushed
past the early-morning caller, crossed the room, and spoke
over her shoulder, "I am ready to go down now."

"Ah, but I am not!" In what seemed but a single step,
the man was beside her and had pinned both arms in his
strong hands in a viselike grip. "I will not be deterred this
time. You will either accept my offer of marrriage or I shall
withdraw it."

Veronica tried to free her arms, but the long fingers
tightened their grip. "Please—" she begged, "you are
hurting me. I—I can't think like this. You are taking advantage of me—of us all—pushing me—us—into a corner.
This is the the 1980s—not the Middle Ages when women
were promised by their parents—"

Involuntarily, Veronica felt cold fingers grip her heart
that inflicted a pain far greater than the fingers that
gripped her arms. Why, that is exactly what her father
had done in one sense of the word. He had extracted a
promise. And her mother—no, she mustn't blame Mother!
It was her own integrity that would compel her to live
up to what was expected of her. Why, then, did the pain
persist?

Veronica's legs suddenly would no longer support her.
"Please, Mr. Devonshire—please, can't we sit down?"

"Indeed, that is what I had hoped for." And, although
the fingers around her arms relaxed, Holman Devonshire

did not let go. Instead, he steered her to the blue-velveted
loveseat in the alcove overlooking the bay. Politely, he
seated her at one end and moved to the other end to seat
himself before speaking.

"Now, first things first. You are not to address me as
'Mr. Devonshire.' "

Veronica stiffened. If this man thought for one minute
she was going to call him *count*! Angered, she again missed
some of the words when he resumed talking. Something
to do with his background. Lord. Marquises. Viscounts,
Dukes. Noblemen. Well, let the egotist boast. To her, titles
meant nothing. And neither did the impossible man wearing this one so proudly.

"—answer to that."

Shaken, Veronica jumped. Her movement seemed to
surprise Holman Devonshire. In a voice that was grim
with strain, she said, "I can't—not without further time.
What you're asking is too much too soon."

Holman Devonshire sighed. "Veronica, dear Veronica,
do you *never* listen? It should not take you an extended
time to decide whether to call me by my Christian name."

Veronica felt color move up from her neck to stain
her cheeks hotly. Obviously, the man prided himself on
outwitting others. If only she had more experience deal-
ing with such men. But the truth was that she had had no
experience with men. Period. Mother was right. Men
were not attracted to her. Even now, she had missed
her cue and Holman Devonshire was speaking in her
place.

"I was explaining," he said hurriedly, "that the titles
have no great amount of meaning. However," he continued, pausing significantly at points, "since it was you
who brought the matter up. . .I shall tell you that. . .yes,
should we be married. . .you, my dear, will become the
Contiesse de Devonshire, because of my Continental
nobility—"

"Whatever are you talking about—" Veronica whispered hoarsely, "what matter did I bring up?" He didn't mean—he couldn't mean—

But he did. "Why, our marriage, your asking a postponement of an answer. Shall we say until this evening then? And would you prefer preceding me to the terrace where we are to breakfast? We would not wish your mother—"

"My mother does not go downstairs. She has a tray in her room."

"Your mother," Holman Devonshire said flatly, "*is* downstairs. Fully dressed. And full of chatter. She has filled me in on your background. It comes as no surprise to me that your mother's ancestors were among the elect who came to America on the *Mayflower*—"

"Correction!" Veronica, angered at him and her mother, spat out. "They were aboard the flagship, the *Santa Maria,* with Christopher Columbus! There *were* a few observers, you know."

Holman Devonshire's eyes narrowed slightly as if he were seeing her anew. "What do you know? The lady does have a sense of humor," he marveled as if to himself. "Yes, she will do nicely as the *contiesse* of Castle Loma."

Veronica scrambled to her feet. She had been insulted quite enough. But why struggle against such a beast? Without a word, she crossed the full length of the room and reached for the heavy brass doorknob. But immediately the man who had invaded and conquered was at her side, his hand on hers as if it took two persons to turn the knob!

Loathing him, and hating herself for the warm shock that began at her fingertips, ran the length of her arm, and threatened to lodge in her heart, Veronica fumbled with the knob beneath his hand. Just a casual contact and she would behave like this! What had happened to her poise?

Her composure? Her senses? This man had come to destroy them too. Her father was right. A *pirate!*

"You need not be afraid, Veronica. I have no intention of harming you." She could feel his warm breath on the back of her neck, its movement sending tendrils of her fine hair from beneath the coil on top. But his voice this time, to her relief, was detached. Then, in contradiction, the tone changed. "I only wished to detain you long enough to say that you are blessed with a lovely figure— too thin, of course—but it has a certain charm. You are one of the few women who should wear pants!"

Another qualification, she thought bitterly. Well, it wouldn't happen again. Not in her room—hers until she could vacate it. If she did—if she *could.* There would be no need to contact Thurman Shield again. The attorney had done all he could do. But Veronica determined to try to talk with Dr. Gillian, seek his advice, ask some questions she had never dared ask before about Mother. And, yes, she needed to see the Reverend Crussell, too. Ask him about—about such a marriage. And how he felt such empty vows would stand up in the eyes of God. It was a big order, all to be done in one day, in addition to the two tours. If this impossible man ever let go of her hand!

"I should have listened to my father about you. He cautioned me about you—" Veronica choked.

Holman Devonshire sounded perplexed. "Too bad he couldn't have known me before passing judgment. Isn't that in violation of one of the cardinal rules of Christianity?"

It was Veronica's turn to be surprised, an emotion which must have registered on her face.

"Ah, yes, I know something of the Church. Fact is that I studied for the priesthood—but then, you have made it clear that my background is of no consequence to you. But tell me, wouldn't it have come as a surprise to your

father to know of my proposal of marriage? Terms of
which we must discuss this evening."

With those words, he let go of her hand. Unknowingly,
she had been pulling with such strength that once her hand
was freed, she fell against him. To her amazement, the
man did not take advantage of the situation. Instead, he
opened the door with a flourish and she fled down the
stairs, her heart pounding unmercifully.

● ● ●

Between the two tours, Veronica telephoned both Dr.
Gillian and the Reverend Crussell. Yes, both men could
drop by and talk with her, they said. Relief swept over
her. Surely, her father's two friends would have wise
words of counsel.

When the doctor came, Veronica ushered him quickly
into the library. Pulling aside the drapes, she quickly
bolted the door, taking the elderly man by surprise.

"I wish there were more time to explain," she said hurriedly, "but I expect Reverend Crussell soon—"

Kindly, he waved away any further explanation and she
was able to get to the matter quickly. "Doctor," she said,
"I have never been quite sure what happened that night—
the night of Mother's fall—and I need to know just how
responsible my father and I are. Can you tell me?"

"I wish I were able to help you." Dr. Gillian ran
a weathered hand across his chin thoughtfully. "Nobody will ever know for sure, I guess. Just another
of those mysteries surrounding the Castle Loma, so
the villagers say! It was storming that night and the
telephones weren't working. Your father came for
me on horseback and how the two of us made it back
alive is one of God's miracles. Eleanore was irrational
and disoriented after the fall. It was hard to tell how

much was fatigue in her state of anxiety."

"Like blaming Father?"

"That—and the idea that her mother's jewels were missing."

Veronica sat erect. This part was news. But that was all the doctor seemed to know about the mystery. He went on to mention what she already knew. She herself had been away at school, but Gil was at home. The quarrel—at least, the quarrel her mother insisted had occurred—came up over the two children. Gilbert had been drinking heavily, a habit her father found disgusting. As they tried to settle matters, the boy himself had come home in a drunken stupor. And from that point, everyone's mind seemed muzzy. Only Eleanore Rosemead claimed to have the corner on truth, he said, which was that Hugh Rosemead had pushed her deliberately in the presence of their son... leaving her helpless at the foot of the stairs... but for the help of the servants. And of course, if Veronica were any kind of daughter, she would be at home helping to serve as hostess as a daughter ought. Small wonder no eligible young man ever looked at the girl twice. . . .

Veronica winced in pain at the memory. Then she put it all behind. She would help Mother as best she could no matter what the truth behind the story was. Unless the doctor possibly knew something. . . .

"Is there no doctor anywhere—any we haven't tried?"

The doctor consulted his watch before answering. "Hugh went through all that, my child," he said tiredly. "But who can say about human flesh—or, for that matter, spirit?"

Dr. Gillian rose to go. "Just one more question—" Veronica rose with him but found herself unable to ask the one question that she felt disloyal to think, let alone put into words.

"Something is troubling you, Veronica. In my practice, I

have learned that it is wiser to discuss one's problems than cover them—especially from ourselves," her father's friend encouraged.

Which was what she had done for years, of course. "Well, then—" she said hesitantly, "is the paralysis all physical—I mean—?"

"You mean could your mother walk if she wished? It's hardly that simple," the doctor said thoughtfully. "No," he decided, "she couldn't walk, not now. But given the right conditions—something which would give her total confidence—" Dr. Gillian spread his hands to show the possibility.

Veronica nodded, her heart heavy. *Something to give her total confidence.* Like her daughter's marrying a man she loathed in order for the family to remain at the Castle Loma. Well, what had she hoped for? Admittedly, the impossible. Something which would nullify her father's request. If it were no longer necessary, she would not have broken a promise, would she? The answer didn't matter now. The hands on the clock were moving toward evening. The answer she must give tonight would have to come from her, not some circumstance. Her alone. Her lips but not her heart.

At the door, Dr. Gillian's tired blue eyes looked into her own. "Your mother tells me that the new owner is much more than she had hoped for, of good background. Mother, upper-class American. Father, European?"

"Probably Bohemian!" Veronica said with feeling, then lowering her voice to its usual soft tone, "My mother and the new proprietor seem to have exchanged confidences— by some strange alliance."

"Is it true that you are considering marriage as your mother says?"

The doctor's question, so gently put, came at a time when she needed to talk. Very much she needed to talk. And suddenly she had told him the whole story in quick, hushed tones. When she finished, he had but one comment.

"It is sad that you alone are the sacrificial lamb," he said sadly. "I am sure that your father never deliberately partook of sour grapes in order to set your teeth on edge. But that is what happened, isn't it? Oh, you poor child!"

He brushed her cheek with his lips, let himself out, and walked slowly toward his ancient-model car in the circular drive. He wanted to help, but—like her—he was helpless.

There was just enough time to order tea carried up to Mother before the minister's appointment. But when Veronica spoke to Hilda, the housekeeper said that Mrs. Rosemead and Count Devonshire were having tea on the balcony overlooking the east garden. . . .

Joseph Crussell listened to Veronica's abridged story of her father's dying request, arrival of "the gentleman who owns Castle Loma," and his proposal. The minister made no comment as she talked, but seemed to concentrate on adjusting his rimless spectacles unnecessarily.

"Isn't this a bit unusual in this day and age?" he asked at length.

Admittedly yes. But would he perform the ceremony—if, indeed, she saw fit to enter into the contract—?

"Contract?" The Reverend Crussell stopped fumbling with his glasses and fixed inquisitive gray eyes on her face.

Veronica felt herself color. She hadn't intended to use the word—had she? If not, what was her purpose for asking the man here this afternoon? Her tired mind seemed to go in unrewarding circles.

Drawing a deep breath, she explained that the marriage would be in name only. A contract, binding but impersonal.

"Are you telling me then that the marriage would not be consummated?" There was surprise on his face.

Veronica dropped her eyes shyly. This was a delicate matter, one she did not discuss with her own mother. It was impossible to talk freely about anything so personal with an outsider.

But when, at length, her guest had not spoken, Veronica knew that he was awaiting an answer. Tremulously, she nodded.

"In all my years of service to the Lord," the minister said slowly, "I have never encountered this kind of situation. What is it you wish of me, Veronica? To perform the ceremony—or do you want advice?"

"Both perhaps," she admitted.

He hesitated. "I'm not sure about either of your needs. Advice I shall withhold at this point—other than to think this thing through. Do nothing impetuous. Pray about this matter—"

"Oh, I have!" Veronica said desperately. "But there has been no answer."

"Maybe that *is* the answer," he offered kindly. "But no, I can see that you want something more. Something immediate."

"I must give an answer tonight."

"Why?"

How could she answer? She didn't know. She knew only that Holman Devonshire had made the demand and, if she did not meet it, he would withdraw his offer. The minister shook his head as if to clear it.

"Strange, but thank you for being honest with me. As to my performing the ceremony, may I ask if this man has been married?"

Veronica blushed and admitted that she did not know. The smile he gave her was kind. "Maybe you should ask your mother!"

Veronica answered his smile, feeling no offense. The elderly minister touched her hand gently. "Other than that, yes, I will do the honors. My reason being that I loved your father very much and held him in high regard. There were times when I wished that he had confided in me as you have done—times when—but never mind that. Set a date—I assume that he will insist on a hasty marriage since that seems to be his manner?''

Veronica murmured that she did not know but—. When she stopped hesitantly, Joseph Crussell asked if something more troubled her. Well—yes—

''Reverend Crussell,'' she all but whispered, ''is what I am considering *wrong*? I mean, in the eyes of God? I have promised my father and feel bound by that, but what about God's expectations for a marriage? I—I—'' She stopped then, unable to continue because of tears.

''Oh, my child,'' he said kindly, ''my heart bleeds for you. I can see that you have agonized over this. And I have no answer. I know that the vows would be empty and meaningless—not the way God intends the union between husband and wife to be, in my opinion. But *wrong*? Sinful? When it is in name only? I don't know—''

He stopped when Veronica's tears became sobs. At length, he said gently, ''Veronica, let me pray about the matter, too. But, in parting, may I say that this situation is not without hope? You know, I have performed a lot of marriage ceremonies in my 50 years in the ministry and I have as yet to have one fail! Who knows but that this one could have a happy ending?''

''Impossible!'' The word came out angrily, an emotion she suddenly appreciated because it stopped her flow of tears.

The month of April seemed to have dried its tears, too. Tomorrow the nation would set its clocks forward, losing or gaining an hour, depending on how one looked at it. Veronica chose to think of it as losing, as she thought of all else these days. She wished she could think of it differently. She needed the extra hour to consider the unsolvable problem facing her. That she was the loser either way there could be no doubt.

This she was thinking, as she walked with Holman Devonshire along the lantana-bordered path leading to the gazebo. The evening air was heady with the scent of orange blossoms and filled with the sound of mockingbird song. An infant moon, almost invisible, seemed to rock its silver cradle above the rhythmic motion of the white-capped waves of the sea. Veronica forgot momentarily the purpose of the walk and let her being throb in keeping with nature's heartbeats.

When a pert little bird flew down to perch on a mimosa tree branch immediately above their heads, Holman Devonshire touched Veronica's arm in signal to stop. Enchanted, she listened as the little creature poured out to the world his gladness—and perhaps his heartaches. So beautiful. So achingly sweet. Almost romantic. And so wasted on the two of them!

She was about to move on when the man put a warning finger to his lips. The little mockingbird's song had changed from one of imitation to a message of its own. It was different, personal. Triumphant. Nothing—*nothing*—the notes promised could not be overcome.

Veronica looked at the man beside her questioningly. That he would find pleasure in the song of a bird surprised her; but he, too, seemed to have understood. "The chap's had a hard day," he whispered, "probably spoiled by some careless mortal. But he has been victorious."

"Our state bird," Veronica offered.

Holman Devonshire nodded. " 'Gay mockingbird who, vocal and joyous mounts on silvered wings, and fulfills the moonlit night with rich melodies.' "

"William Bartram, American naturalist." Veronica responded from her father's training.

The singing went on as his two enemies, or friends, passed beneath the blossom-strung branch upon which he perched. At the gazebo, Holman Devonshire politely took

Veronica's arm, escorted her up the short flight of steps to the landing, and waited until she was seated before bursting out, "What is your answer?"

The question, so sudden from the man standing above her—a totally different man than the one with whom she had enjoyed a moment's bird song and exchange of pleasure in words—caught her by surprise. Immediately, her heart pounded against her rib cage and drummed against her eardrums. Was it possible that he could hear the wild beating?

"Couldn't this wait? Must I rush into a marriage? It's a big step—" Veronica hated herself for faltering. Oh, why hadn't she rehearsed?

"No!" The word was so emphatic that it was frightening. "I have stated my terms. I know you do not love me or even wish to marry me. Our feelings for one another are closely aligned on that matter, except that I need a hostess, a wife who is neither stupid nor meddlesome. Nothing more is required. You, your charming but rather self-serving mother, and ne'er-do-well brother may remain here. You may go your way and I shall most certainly go mine. As I see it, you would be getting the better of the bargain!"

Veronica's voice sounded hollow in her own ears. The gazebo was a stage. She was a puppet dangling helplessly on a set of strings, none of which she could control. "How do I know you will stick by your promises?"

"You don't."

"Oh, I hate you! I *hate* you!" Veronica cried out, using the word for the first time in her life. But, then, she had never been so angry, so humiliated. So helpless. "My father was right—"

"Your father was always 'right' from all reports. In all matters. So let us assume that he was right in extracting a promise from you which will afford me with a suitable nominal wife."

"Nominal. In name only. You promise?"

"I have already promised. And you have questioned my pledge. Let's resolve the matter by saying it is conditional. There are certain expectations I have. Call them promises if you will. And as long as you keep those conditions, I shall keep mine."

"What are your conditions?" Her voice was but a bitter whisper in the gathering dusk. Knotting her handkerchief into a ball, she waited, every muscle aching with tension.

Holman Devonshire seated himself in the chair opposite her. "Veronica, I am not remotely interested in you or your love. Why would I impose myself upon you? You have a certain charm, somewhat like the pieces in this mansion—a lovely collector's item but lacking in warmth. You compliment it nicely and I shall be proud to display you. Nothing more. Those are my terms. Yours are to be a gracious hostess *always,* serving—for all the world knows—as my devoted wife in *more* than name. Is that understood?"

Mutely, Veronica nodded.

"And," he continued in a cold voice, "I shall have to ask that you do not disclose the terms of our agreement." When she nodded again, he added, "Now, there is one more thing I shall expect, *albeit,* demand! That you do not at any point question me concerning my private life. It is none of your business at this point."

I don't care what your private life is! Veronica longed to cry out. Instead, she gulped in a breath of the blossom-drenched night air and whispered. "I have no choice, have I?"

"None that I see. So is it agreed?"

Defeated and ashamed, she nodded, unaware that the night lights which had come on automatically around the eaves of the gazebo tangled in her silver-blonde hair like stars. The man across from her, his face hidden by the shadows of the hibiscus branches, was very much aware.

"Very well," he said tersely. "I shall have my attorney draw up the papers."

"Is that necessary?"

"It is very necessary. So if you have any further requests?"

"Will I be allowed to continue the tours—I mean for my personal money?"

"Your life is your own as I have told you. But, as for the money, I will take care of that. I am a man of means. Anything more?"

"There are certain heirlooms—"

"We shall inventory together. Now?"

But Veronica had one more question. "I-I would like to have the worship services on Sunday—" She paused, not sure she could go on.

He shrugged. "Your spiritual life, as well as your private life, are your own affair. Now, have you found me unreasonable?"

Veronica could think of no suitable way to respond. Just why the intruder wanted a wife was a mystery, unless her respectability was some sort of cover-up. But she would keep her promises to him as she was keeping her promise to her father. The stakes were too high to risk losing!

She retired at the usual time. Maybe it was because of the extra hour that sleep was impossible. Untrue, of course. Insomnia came from confusion and an anger at almost everyone around her. Try as she would to pray, the words felt like empty phrases. So she lay dry-eyed and wide awake as the clocks in the various halls chimed the slowly-passing hours. She was about to doze, it seemed, when there was a strange, shuffling noise directly above her head. Sitting erect, Veronica tried to identify the sound. Had it come from the attic where so many of the collections were stored? Her father had planned to expand, to add another wing—

What *was* the noise? To her annoyance, her heart picked up the message and beat faster, making it impossible to tell just where it came from. Maybe it wasn't in the attic, after all. She wondered for the first time just where Count Holman Devonshire had chosen to make his headquarters. The idea was disturbing, so she crept out of bed and checked to be sure the dead-bolt was secured. Finally, she slept . . . .

• • •

One week later, Veronica Lea Rosemead became the Contiesse de Devonshire. Veronica, to her mother's dismay, chose to wear the single long, black gown she had bought for mourning—velvet with a wide lace collar which was most becoming but unlikely for a wedding dress. She allowed Hilda to force an enormous bouquet of crimson roses and maiden hair ferns into her arms but refused to go into the village to have her hair done.

"It would not stay in, Mother, as you should know," she defended when Eleanore Rosemead chided her.

"You will never make a suitable wife," her mother said in despair.

Veronica heard no more. She would never be a suitable anything in her mother's eyes. Another failure was to be expected.

She repeated the words said by the Reverend Crussell in a voice that was grim with strain. Once or twice she faltered and was surprised when Holman Devonshire filled in with deeply-intoned words, holding lightly to her arm to support her trembling body.

After the cake and punch which, to her surprise, was unspiked as she had requested because of Gilbert's addiction, she and her new husband drove away in the black limousine Holman Devonshire had engaged from the village. A sapphire-blue diamond "of Hope" flashed mockingly on the third finger of Veronica's left hand.

To the few who had witnessed the empty vows, the two of them may have looked for all the world like the happy bride and groom. Veronica had tossed her bouquet obediently over the banister of the curving staircase as she left to don a casual bone-linen suit for traveling. The groom had brushed her cheek with a dutiful kiss and they had smiled for a photograph . . . with mutual hatred in their hearts, Veronica was sure. Her empty heart said, "Charade of Love. . . ."

Once they were on their way somewhere, where not mattering, she burst into tears. The man beside her was her *husband!* This should have been a night of dreams-come-true. Not the nightmare it was . . . .

Chapter 5

Holman Devonshire had arranged that his new bride should have shopping time in Miami before the two of them boarded a luxury liner for a honeymoon cruise of the Florida Keys. Veronica watched, as a parade of models showed clothing in one of the city's most exclusive salons. She selected a white five-piece ensemble with a series of interesting button-down skirts, pants, and coulette and contrasting tops "all coordinated for *madame's* exquisite coloring." When Veronica would have chosen long sleeves because of her tendency to burn in the sometimes merciless sun, she was encouraged to purchase matching parasols instead—"so *elegante*, like *madame* herself!"

Her husband, carefully attentive, watched with Veronica, occasionally speaking in French to the head of the shop and to Veronica directly when she selected a slim princess-line, street-length dinner dress, its scopped neckline made demure by the row of double ruffles around it. "You are blessed with good taste, my dear. The color is the exact shade of your eyes."

"We call it *pheure bleue*," the hovering proprietress whispered in approval. "Eees beau-*ti*-ful!"

Holman Devonshire frowned. "The 'hour blue,' " he translated.

Veronica could see that he was no longer pleased. Well, she was. She liked the understated simplicity of the dress and, if she must dress according to standards, at least she could choose her own color. And "blue hour" was appropriate.

But something bothered her. Something lying deep inside which had to do with choices...oh, yes, she remembered. And remembering, she automatically lifted a hand to her throat where the throbbing began. Holman Devonshire saw and she read a question in his eyes.

"The contract," she whispered. "Wasn't I supposed to sign one?"

"Veronica," his low tone carried a note of exasperation, "Of all the inopportune times—but yes, one will catch up with us aboard ship. My lawyer will be meeting us at Key West since it seems so important to you."

Veronica started to reply hotly that it was of no consequence to her whatsoever but that she had thought he was the one...then asked herself, *What's the use?* and turned back to the shopping. She purchased a few other garments she felt would make her "presentable" and no amount of insistence on the part of her husband or the enterprising French lady could lead her into an elaborate wardrobe. She was going to remain as unindebted to this man as was possible. Her promise was to keep up appearances. Nothing more.

Once aboard ship, Veronica learned that The Count and Countess Holman de Devonshire were to occupy the honeymoon suite, the grandest of them all. That added to the mockery. But she would play his little game. After all, this pantomime was to last only one week and then she would be back on familiar ground. Here she would be the blushing bride. There she would be the charming hostess. But deep in her heart, Veronica was convinced that Holman Devonshire had more to gain by the sham. Her father, harsh as he was in his assessment of those who failed to meet his standards, could not be that far wrong about this man. The fact that he had robbed her brother was proof enough. She would be as meek as a lamb on the surface, but she would be as sly as a fox, watching, waiting. One day he would say a word or make a move that would betray himself. Then, somehow, she would regain Castle Loma and her self-respect. . .she could wait. . . .

Veronica saw little of her husband during the cruise. He spent a great deal of time away from their chambers—undoubtedly in the gambling casinos. When the ship docked, it was he who went ashore on unexplained journeys. Not that she cared. Veronica was surprised to find herself enjoying the peacefulness of lying in a deck chair, her face almost obscured by enormous blue-lensed sunglasses. Watching the water change its moods. Drinking in the sunrises and sunsets. Feeling the warmth of the life-giving sun through her sunscreen. It was here that she prayed and felt that her words were no longer empty. They were conversations with her Creator. She did not try to excuse herself to God. She asked His understanding instead. And finally, she prayed that somehow she could bring something from this meaningless marriage that would be more worthy in His eyes than it was in her own.

Veronica had always been a person of solitude. She was grateful that the prying eyes which followed the count and countess or the knowing glances that people somehow seem to reserve for newlyweds did not follow her when she was alone. *That figured,* she thought ironically, *like Mother says, I never stand out—by myself. I just fade into the woodwork unnoticed.* But aboard ship , that was rewarding!

In the dining room, it was different. At first, Veronica

had pleaded that she be allowed to dine in her room. Holman Devonshire had won his point easily when he said that she might do so on one condition. He would dine with her. "The privacy might be nice. . . " And he had smiled.

Once she became accustomed to the distant manner of the waiter, the head waiter visiting their secluded table to check at regular intervals, and the audience that watched their every move, Veronica came to forget her surroundings and enjoy the cuisine. When she looked hopelessly at some of the menus, her husband smiled indulgently—for their audience, she was sure—and translated for her. Soon she learned that *antipasti misti al'Italiana* was simply a selection of Italian hors d'oeuvres; *zuppa di scarola* was chicken consomme with escargot (snails, she believed?), and *gelato cassata* was ice cream supreme.

"I thought you had been abroad," he teased, aware of watchful eyes.

A little embarrassed, Veronica dropped her eyes—demure, that's the way a bride should be, the eyes of the audience said.

"I have, but only briefly—certainly not long enough to master the Italian language."

"Some day perhaps we shall travel there together."

How false could this man be! Anger made her blush even more. And she dared not raise her eyes for fear they would reveal her emotions. Make a scene. Against the rules. *Lovely,* the audience told one another.

The groom, the "royalty watchers" observed, leaned intimately near his blushing bride. The words he said were, "Keep it up, my dear. You are playing the game as I had hoped. You are giving the tourists a romantic picture to take home to their ascetic lives!"

Veronica tilted her head a little lower, letting the breeze from the open porthole pick up her hair as it strayed in undisciplined tendrils at the back of her neck. "Like me?"

Veronica knew that his eyes followed her fingers as she traced the pattern on the crystal bud vase that centered their table, wanting her to lift her eyes. But she did not.

With a sigh that she was sure was born of boredom, Holman spoke the fatal words. "Exactly like you, my dear Veronica. Perhaps burning with secret desires but conditioned to behave as one should. Destined to live a life of quiet desperation."

Humiliated, Veronica drew her elbows up to rest them on the table. Then, cupping her hands, she eased her chin into her damp palms.

The effect was charming, of course. They were such a pair! So the people went on watching as the maitre d' hotel came to light a candle in the squat, rose-colored glass bubble that encased it. Veronica raised her great, blue eyes to thank him, and the lights from the candle caught in their depths. She refused dessert but stood obediently for their audience. Her husband took her elbow, every eye watching their idols. In the hall the show ended. She tore her arm away and rushed down the stairs, refusing to wait for an elevator. In the privacy of her room she sat down and, without turning on a light, gazed unseeingly at the placid water. *I am paying the price now, Holman Devonshire,* her heart cried out, *but you will pay later. That is my promise to myself!*

Before she drifted into a troubled sleep, Veronica thought she heard noises in the adjoining room which her husband occupied for appearance sake. One of them sounded angry— gruff and threatening. Yes, she was sure it was her husband's voice, although it was low-pitched, which answered. Then there was profanity . . . the shuffling of chairs . . . a crash . . . followed by the opening and closing of a door. Then silence.

Well, one thing for certain, was her last thought: The cruise had prepared her for married life. What was expected of her and how to react. And what she could expect from the unscrupulous man to whom she was wedded.

It was no better and no worse than she had expected. . . .

In Key West, Holman Devonshire announced that he would be going ashore to bring back the lawyer. Veronica was to remain in her room, order room service to bring tea, and be prepared to "receive."

Nothing she could have done would have prepared Veronica to receive the man who appeared some two hours later when her husband rapped on the door of her stateroom. The tea service was laid out and Veronica, showered and coiffed, wore one of the striped silk sport dresses she had purchased in Miami. She looked the part of the perfect hostess. But she did not play the part well.

"My dear," Holman Devonshire said smoothly, "may I present my attorney, Mr. Thurman Shield?"

Thurman! Veronica felt her face blanch. She was aware dimly that her friend took her hand warmly when her husband said, "My wife, the Contiesse de Devonshire," and that his gray eyes were as surprised as hers must be. His face was so ashen it matched his silvery hair. She knew that they were being watched, but there was no undoing what had been done.

The rest of the meeting was a horrible dream. She heard nothing and signed obediently where she was told, smearing her signature badly.

When Thurman Shield murmured, "It is quite all right, Mrs. Devonshire," Veronica remembered that she had tensed. But, to her immense relief, her husband did not correct him. Oh, surely that must mean that he was not going to insist upon that pretentious title. . . .

Oh, there was another copy to be signed? She hadn't known, she murmured, and leaned down to write carefully. Forcing her eyes to focus lest she sign this copy badly, Veronica sighted something that she had not been able to read before. A single line above the place for affixing their signature read: "We, the undersigned, neither of whom has been wedded previously and having no legal heirs. . . " She read no more. That answered the question the minister had asked. Only he had failed to mention it again. Not that it mattered. Nothing did. Nothing at all. . . .

● ● ●

Veronica Devonshire took up her duties at Castle Loma. But it was a different Veronica than the one who had managed the household before the property was taken from the Rosemead family. The marriage vows were empty and meaningless. And yet something was changed. She had been a girl. She was now a woman. There was no explaining it, not even to herself.

The entire household changed as well. Holman Devonshire needed nobody to tell him that the place was badly in need of repair. He set to work immediately seeking the carpenters and painters they would need. The place was understaffed. Hilda could use more help and certainly James needed a full-time gardener. As to other details, "I will know better when I accompany you on tours," he told Veronica.

The guest dining room was first on the itinerary the morning the new owner accompanied Veronica. She knew of his plans and wondered if he expected to be introduced and, if so, how she should go about it. Holman Devonshire, however, remained unobtrusively at the end of the line. None of the guests knew that he was among the spectators, larger in number now that Castle Loma was the property of "royalty," "foreigners," and a few other choice adjectives which reached Veronica's ears through Hilda.

"Folks whisper," the head housekeeper confided after one of her shopping trips to the village, "that there are wild goings-on atop Enchanted Hill. Some of the talk originates, if you will pardon my tongue, ma'am—" The middle-aged woman hesitated and then supplied another title, "Or should I say 'Madame' or 'Countess'? It is perplexing and I want to please His Highness—"

Veronica forced a smile at the woman who had undoubtedly assisted Dr. Gillian in bringing her into the sheltered world atop the steep hill—as much a "mountain" as the state of Florida afforded and certainly the site of greatest grandeur. "I always liked 'Miss Veronica'—"

Hilda's eyes widened in horror. "Oh, no, that would never do!"

"Then 'ma'am' if you insist, but no title—in spite of what the new owner may have told you!" she said with feeling.

"Oh, no! His Majesty has been most kind and I am sure you know that his generosity is beyond our hopes."

Veronica did not know, but she was glad. Hilda and James had been a loyal pair, remaining when the small fortune dwindled. She thought it best, however, that the household help be given no inkling of the arrangement with her husband. Instead, she turned the conversation back to what Hilda was about to say concerning the origin of the village gossip.

"Oh, that—" Hilda tried to wave it away with her hand. "It is only hearsay, you know, but Mr. Gilbert does—well—tend to be talkative when he has a few too many. And the talk spreads at the Sea Oats. Oh, would that he did not patronize that evil place—"

When Hilda hesitated, Veronica knew the housekeeper wanted to say more. She should put an end to the conversation. But maybe there was something more she needed to know. A word of encouragement was all it took for Hilda to divulge what she knew. That the place was heavily into illegal lotteries and gambling. Did Miss Veronica— *Mrs. Devonshire, pardon ma'am*—know that there was a large floating casino, a brilliantly-lighted floating vessel which, under the disguise of a dining-dancing harbor-sightseeing boat, sailed out into international waters to gamble?

"And my brother is among them?" Veronica had asked.

Well, talk was—but there the woman stopped. It was then that Holman Devonshire had walked in yesterday to inquire about the timing of today's excursions. She prayed that he had not overheard . . . it would be just like him to eavesdrop, a small offense compared to all else he had done to her life . . . .

When all the guests had assembled on the marble landing at the front of the main building, Veronica eyed the crowd in dismay. She should divide the guests into at least two groups. Gilbert knew every inch of Castle Loma and could be very charming when he chose. She considered asking the guests to wait just a moment while she went in search of her brother. Then she remembered with a sick heart the sound of his dragging footsteps just as dawn streaked her bedroom window with a first pink light.

Organizing as best she could, after a brief somewhat self-conscious welcome, Veronica led the guests into the cathedral-like dining room. She called attention to the ceiling which was imported, according to her father's reports, from a sixteenth-century monastery in Italy. As they exchanged gasps over the bigger-than-life figures of the saints of the Renaissance carved on the great dome above, Veronica let her eyes search the monastic room for her husband. She caught his eyes looking straight back into her own, his face wearing an unmistakable expression of pride. Well, let him be proud—proud as a peacock—if he could find pleasure in robbing, stealing, and swindling! Small wonder he needed a lawyer.

With that thought, unresolved questions surfaced in her mind. How did he come to know Thurman Shield? She had considered him *her* friend. How could he be and yet be retained—

Holman Devonshire's expression changed. He seemed to be signaling . . . and with a start she realized that her guests were waiting to move on, their necks tired from looking up. She herself had spent many rainy-day hours studying the beautiful artwork, wondering which saint each figure represented until she learned them all. But guests never had the time or the interest. A casual glance and they were ready to move on. With a sigh, she moved on to point out the 75 fold-down chairs, carved with cherubs and infant angels.

Why 75? "My father was not a superstitious man," Veronica smiled. "But he never wished to embarrass his guests. He felt that if he had an odd number, nobody would feel like the proverbial 'fifth wheel.' Ladies need not be escorted unless they chose. And in any case, the extra chair was my father's way of welcoming the wayfaring stranger into the household—no matter who he was—"

She caught her husband's eyes again and blushed under their mocking smile. Her father's welcome-chair did not hold an invitation to him, they both knew. Determinedly, she turned back to the tourists.

Did they wish to spend more time with the paintings? But no, guests were already craning their collective necks to see the artifacts at the end of the great room. Walking regretfully past the oil paintings of St. Peter and St. Paul keeping watch over the long, massive table, Veronica moved to the ceiling-high shelves which displayed carved, gold leaf bowls, Grecian urns, and exquisite statues, centered by a marble carving of the "Madonna and Child" modeled after the original painting, and the large collection of Bibles.

"It seems that the owner, this Mr. Rosemead, must have been a very religious man" an anonymous voice observed from the crowd.

"Yes, my father was indeed a devout man," Veronica answered. "He always said that was his *soul* purpose," she paused hoping that the play on words would need no explaining, saw it was hopeless, and—wishing she had not bothered—tried to make her meaning clear. All of which was lost on unhearing ears. She ended in mid-sentence and offered an example instead.

"You can see the Christian overtones here in the medieval art. I especially want to call your attention to—"

Veronica heard her voice trail away in shock. The gold-encrusted cross, one of the most valuable collection pieces not under lock and key was gone! Trying to regain her self-control, she pointed out the tapestries woven with varying sizes of the Mother and Child which adorned the multipaned windows. Then, inviting the guests to have coffee on their way out and visit the souvenir shop in the vestibule if they wished, she hurried out to greet the next group. . . .

The place was so filled with workmen that Veronica often had to change schedules during the busy weeks that followed. Veronica was torn between the need of sitting down with Holman Devonshire and setting up an inventory before other items of value disappeared and her wish to avoid him at all costs. What was there to say to a man like him? And most certainly she did not trust him . . . so wouldn't it be foolish, maybe even dangerous, to let him know that she was aware that the cross was missing? Obviously, he was responsible.

Between tours and taking care of Mother, Veronica conferred with the decorator her husband had brought in from Miami. Together they selected new fabrics, in keeping with the worn materials but enough lighter-toned to give a lift to the otherwise somber walls and furniture. Russet to apricot. Maroon to dusty-rose. Olive to celery. "And surely *madame* would wish her bedroom reorganized to reflect her many moods?" The Frenchman spoke rapidly. "Something—ah, yes, romantic—a background where she can lounge in satin pajamas, read Colette in French, yes?"

No! Veronica shocked the small, dapper man by saying, a "quiet mood." A retreat. Books and chamber music records. A bit of blue to reflect the sea—and new shelves to hold her collection of shells. . . .

May turned to June and Veronica hardly noticed. Except for the heady scent of a million roses. She had built a world of her own—of sorts. Avoiding showdowns and inevitable answers. And then Holman destroyed her private world, taking it over as he had taken over the Castle Loma in a bloodless revolution.

Later she was to wonder why there was no forewarning in the quiet before the storm. Her mother's sudden placidity. Her husband's preoccupation with papers and documents which had nothing to do with herself. Even her brother's seemingly improved behavior. *But I chose to live in a fool's paradise of blindness,* she thought bitterly. *I should have known that Mother was seeing too much of her son-in-law, letting herself be beguiled by his affable manner. Just as I should have seen the danger signal in the betrayer's too-cool-and-easy manner. And, as for Gilbert. . . .*

"Can't you leave the boy alone! There is no need for your over-concern with money now, Veronica. Let him enjoy his youth, an art you never seemed to master," Mother had said. So, rather than agitate Mrs. Rosemead further, Veronica closed her eyes to the long absences, the deliberate efforts to avoid any confrontation with her, and his obvious tension and restlessness when she encountered him briefly in their mother's presence. . . .

So she was unprepared for Holman Devonshire's knock on her bedroom door that bright morning in mid-June. "Come in!" she called, thinking it was Hilda's "wake-up call," a childhood practice the woman insisted on continuing well after there was any need.

"Good morning, by beautiful wife!" The deeply intoned masculine voice never failed to surprise her, but the man's presence was more than surprising. What's more, he was coming in the door!

Clutching the thin cotton, somewhat faded, floral wrapper about her nightgown, Veronica backed away from the door in alarm. Holman Devonshire closed the door softly and took a step toward her. Quickly, she took a step backward, painfully aware of her disheveled hair which hung in hopelessly fine-as-thistledown strands to her shoulders, the pale blonde strands falling stubbornly over her face like a fan. When she tried to sweep it from her eyes, she lost her balance as one heel caught on the claw-food of an antique table. With a little cry, Veronica reeled dizzily backward.

In an instant, a long arm encircled her waist and righted her position. Caught against the broad hard chest, she gasped with breathless relief, still trembling from the near-fall.

"I'm all right—" But the words ended in an intake of breath. A sharp pain had shot through her right ankle when she tried to put her weight on the foot.

Veronica met his gaze then. The face above hers was filled with concern, the strange eyes lighted by the first rays of the morning sun filtering softly through the sheer glass curtain between the heavy brocade drapes. Then concern turned to something else—something unidentifiable in the burning depths.

"Veronica . . ."

She must move. Only for some reason her senses were reeling. She found herself incapable of moving. Incapable even of speech.

"You must get off the foot," Holman Devonshire whispered huskily. And, without warning, he swept her thinly-clad body up effortlessly and turned toward her unmade bed.

"You-you promised not to enter my room," she whispered weakly.

"Uninvited," he corrected, his mouth almost touching her ear, his breath warm against her cheek.

Seeming to have no will of her own, Veronica relaxed against him. As he leaned to ease her onto the bed, neither of them heard the door swing open without warning.

"Pretty pic-chur!" Gilbert's drunken bellow, the words slurred, broke through Veronica's consciousness.

"What are you doing here?" The words were torn from her throat. Whatever must her brother think! His sister in the arms of this man who had robbed them. Wearing nothing but a flimsy garment. Hair down... barefoot... she tried to pull herself erect.

Gilbert's bloodshot eyes took the whole scene in. "You're just as full of the devil, my bea*uuu*-ti-ful sis-der as th' devil here—"

"Watch it!" Holman Devonshire managed to set her in a sitting position and moved toward the swaying man at the same time. "You are not to speak to my wife in that tone, do you understand?" His voice was low, but there could be no mistaking the threat in its tone.

"Wife—*wife?* Her? Oh, eees fun-*eee*—no wife—just a—a—"

Her husband pinned both of Gilbert's arms against his body with white-knuckled hands. "She's my wife! And she's your sister. You are to treat her with respect. I ought to make you eat those words—I ought to kill you!"

"Go 'head. Wouldn't be first time you murdered—"

From where Veronica sat in speechless horror she saw Holman Devonshire double up a fist menacingly and then drop it. "Get thee behind me, Satan!" he uttered. "What's the use of bloodying up my hands with the likes of you!"

Released, Gilbert swayed on his feet, then with an obvious look of relief, turned to take a staggering step toward the open door. And there, to add to the horror, stood Hilda and James.

"Mr. Gilbert, you are in the wrong room—" James moved to put a steadying hand on Gilbert's arm.

Safely out of his brother-in-law's reach, her brother

turned to look accusingly at Veronica. *"She*, my own trusted sis-der, locked me out—''

''I have a key, Mr. Gilbert,'' Hilda soothed. Then turning to the count, ''I'm sorry, Your Majesty.''

Holman Devonshire straightened his tweed jacket with a quick nervous hand and, smiling at the housekeeper, said, ''There's no problem. And, Hilda, you need not be quite so formal. After all, I am not a king, you know!''

The woman curtsied. Veronica hardly knew whether to be angry or amused. Maybe she would have expressed her displeasure to Holman Devonshire in other circumstances. But, drained as she was emotionally, she found herself bursting into laughter. Curtsy indeed!

Her husband turned to her, a look of pleasure on his face. ''That, my dear, is the first time I have ever heard you laugh. A fringe benefit I never expected.''

Something clicked in Veronica's brain then. The daze lifted. The bitterness of the entire situation came back, multiplying rapidly, filling the room, bursting her heart. Gilbert was gone earlier in the day when she made an effort to see him. The door was not locked. This was not the day for Hilda to have one of her helpers clean the bedroom wing. . . and her brother had accused Veronica of locking him out. . . yes, it all fit. And she had fallen into the trap. A ''fringe benefit'' of this unpardonable caper. . . a laughingstock. . . .

''You arranged this!'' She spoke the horrifying words in a whisper, unable to believe or comprehend, but knowing they were true.

''Yes,'' he said. Nothing more.

''But how could you? What purpose—why would you lead me to believe—*why?*''

Holman Devonshire's voice when he spoke was low and, if she hadn't known his mean nature so well, Veronica would have taken them to be sincere. ''Are you telling me that you wished it were otherwise? That you wish I had visited your room simply to be alone with you? Alone. The two of us?''

"I'm saying nothing of the kind!" Veronica denied hotly, as she fought off the memory of his arms around her and her momentary weakness. Well, she would not be taken in again! "I'm demanding an explanation of your inexcusable behavior—your embarrassing me in the presence of my brother, Hilda and James—"

Whatever gentleness she might have imagined in the man's voice was gone. Her husband's tone was angry. "You are in a position to *demand* nothing. But it so happens that I choose to tell you why I staged the touching scene of man and wife behaving as man and wife are expected to behave. A part of our bargain was that the two of us would, to all outside eyes, *be* man and wife. Remember?''

Numbly, Veronica nodded.

"Well, then, I thought some practice would help. But before I tell you just why the little rehearsal at this particular time, I want you to know that I did not expect you to have an accident—may I have a look at the ankle?''

"You stay away from me!" Veronica hissed. "Don't touch me now or ever again.''

He shrugged. "As you wish." The tone said very plainly that Holman Devonshire did not care. "But," he continued, "yes, I locked the door of your brother's room because I need to have a talk with him, something I have tried to arrange without success. And yes, again—I hoped he would come in so the three of us could talk...Never mind...why burden you with full explanations? It is plain that you would not believe them.''

That was very true, her tight-lipped silence told him.

"And for your information, your playboy brother is now locked *in*side!''

"Gil? Locked in his room? Why, you can't hold him a prisoner in his own house!''

"Whose house?" Holman Devonshire let the words soak in then resumed, "As to the servants how do you think they happened along if not by prearrangement? Gilbert and I will be going over some assets. And now, turning to other matters, this was obviously not a dress rehearsal for the party." There was amusement in his voice.

Party? The word left Veronica speechless.

"Your birthday," he said, responding to the questioning in her face as her naturally-arched brows curved even higher. "It *is* June twenty-first, you know. I should like to have some guests in for the occasion. It is time you met some of my friends."

She had forgotten it was nearing her twenty-fifth birthday. Mother had always pointed them out as unmarried milestones, but there was no need for that now . . . and Father was not here to enjoy the day with her . . . but a party? No! And no to meeting these people, as well.

Veronica was unaware that she was shaking her head until her husband spoke again. "Yes, my dear, there *will* be a party—and you will attend. In fact, you will be the center of attention. It is a matter of record, you know."

Yes, she knew. She knew the terms of the agreement by heart. Every empty, hypocritical word. But she had her pride. This usurper had not robbed her of that any more than her father had allowed life to rob him of his. She was a Rosemead—not a Devonshire!

"What if I refuse your request?"

"It is not a request. It is an order—an order that both of us know you can't afford to refuse. Plans are already underway. Invitations are out. Your dress is ordered. And you will show up if I have to transport you downstairs in one of the packing boxes I found in the attic."

In the attic. So she *had* heard a noise in the attic that night. If she asked questions, the man would remind her again that he held propriety. That he would come and go as he chose. An option which was no longer open to herself or her family.

"What have you done to us?" The words came out dull, flat, and helpless. "You have taken everything we have—made us miserable—"

"Your mother is not at all miserable, quite happy, in fact, as you see evidenced by her bright chatter and presence at the dinner table. The servants are happy—all right, *help* if you prefer," he added when she winced. "I will soon know just what your brother's frame of mind is, among other things. So, you see, my dear, you seem to be the only one who is miserable. Of course, being the modest one, you would not admit to yourself that you are the only one who made a down payment. Let's say that actually the situation is a blessing in disguise, a sort of *coupe de grace,* an act of mercy!"

"You need not translate for me! I may be clumsy, but I know enough French to know the literal meaning of that phrase," Veronica was shaking with anger. "The executioner's death blow to end the suffering of the condemned!"

Holman Devonshire smiled crookedly. *"Touche!"* he said softly. He turned and was about to leave when suddenly he faced her.

"Veronica, there is something more we need to discuss. The inventory, we've not gotten around to that."

"There has been no time," she said quietly, "but it is something we need to go over—before something else turns up missing."

She could have bitten her tongue off. It would have been better left unsaid. She should have kept quiet. To have watched in silence. Until Holman Devonshire made a slip that would prove her father right about him. And in case he was operating illegally. . . .

But he seemed unruffled. "Agreed," he said, as if he were innocent of the matter. Well, that was like him.

"If you will leave, I can get dressed for the day," Veronica kept her voice coldly polite.

Her husband half-saluted and reached for the door-knob. "By the by," he called carelessly over his shoulder, "your mother thinks it is time we started a family, a legal heir, you know." There could be no mistaking his meaning nor had he mistaken her mother's. Well, she was not going to dignify their collaboration—although with far different motives—with any kind of a response.

When he continued to hesitate at the door, Veronica raised her eyes cautiously from the floral pattern in the Persian rug she had been studying. Their eyes locked and the intensity of his gaze in the shadow cast by the door startled her. The look frightened her. Else why would her pulses pound when he looked like that?

"Do you still hate me?"

His question came so suddenly that Veronica was too startled to speak. She stood rooted to the deep pile of the rug like a helpless fledgling hypnotized by a stalking cat. *I am his prey,* she thought numbly. *Whatever he wills—*

"But of course not! That would hardly be in keeping with your plans, would it, my dear?" his voice was gently chiding.

"I don't know what you're talking about—" she gasped, trying to tear her eyes away.

"It is of no consequence," he shrugged. "We go our separate ways, isn't that the way the agreement reads?"

"I—I don't know—you—I—"

Her husband laughed indulgently. "Do you mean to say that you did not read it, just signed on the dotted line—or did you make an *X*?"

Veronica tore her eyes away but was unable to say what she felt. That he was despicable. And yes, she hated him. But regrettably, what he said was true. She hadn't read the papers thrust before her.

With an effort, she brought herself back to the present in order to hear what her captor was saying. "—so you can go over the terms at will. You don't mind if he occupies the office your father used? It is well-stocked with books, but some shelves would serve nicely for *his* books. I'm sure you will welcome his presence."

"Who?" Veronica asked stupidly.

Holman Devonshire shook his head in despair. "One day I will be compelled to lock you in a tower and throw away the key. There I will force you to listen when I speak! A woman who listens has mastered a great skill. I often wonder why the writers didn't include listening in the list of virtues for a good wife."

"*Who*?" she repeated, knowing that the answer was important.

"Authorship of Proverbs is uncertain—"

"*Who*?" Veronica knew that her voice rose shrilly, but she no longer cared. "Who is coming to occupy my father's office?"

"Why, Thurman Shield, my attorney and, I gather, your intimate friend?"

The question hung in the silence of the room as Holman Devonshire closed the door softly behind him.

Chapter 6

Sleep was impossible for the three nights after her husband's visit. The party was scheduled for the following night and Veronica was dimly aware of the air of festivity which suddenly prevailed. Her mother was in the highest of spirits. Her cheeks glowed as if she had indeed bathed in the replica of the legendary Fountain of Youth which dominated the 1200-acre estate. "The count will try the lanterns tonight," Eleanore said excitedly. "Every window in the eighty rooms will glow!" And then she sighed. "I do wish, Veronica, that you would try to show a little more enthusiasm!"

But Veronica was depressed. Depressed, apprehensive—and frightened. The depression she could understand. Undoubtedly it sprang from the deep sense of guilt she carried over the life of deception her husband was forcing her to live. True, she had explained to those closest to her, but how could she make them understand the things she did not understand herself? This hateful party, for instance.

The thought of tomorrow night's party caused Veronica to shiver as she zipped up the pale blue velvet robe. But no matter how she felt, the show must go on. Somehow she knew there would be watchful eyes on her every move. The eyes of his acquaintances, whoever they were. And the eyes of her friends, although they were few in number. Mostly, she thought of Dr. Gillian, the Reverend Crussell—and Thurman Shield.

Thurman! *No wonder I am apprehensive,* Veronica thought as she walked over to open the window, *how could he have accepted an invitation to make his headquarters here? It's like a betrayal. . . or is it a conflict of interest? Isn't he representing two clients?*

Maybe the blue robe was too warm, after all. The open window failed to bring in the garden-fresh breeze Veronica had hoped for. The air was heavy. Clouds were piling up along the horizon and the birds seemed to be sulking. Even the white blossoms on the gardenia hedge looked plastic in their stillness.

Veronica turned from the window and opened the door of one of her closets in search of a cooler garment. There was no need to dwell on questions regarding Thurman's coming to Castle Loma. It was just one of the many unsolved riddles. Small wonder the villagers thought the occupants of this mansion a strange lot. And the mysterious plot thickened with each passing hour. Yes, she was frightened. More so since Thurman was no longer her ally—

In her deep sense of apprehension, a light rap on the bedroom door was startling. Feeling too warm and too cold at the same time, Veronica clutched the velvet robe about her. The knock sounded again.

"Yes?" She hoped her voice did not tremble.

The voice on the other side of the massive door was

muffled and sounded like Hilda's when she cried. Maybe something was wrong with Mother—

Her nervous fingers fumbled with the night latch and dead-bolt. When at last she was able to open the door, she was all but swept off her feet by the enormous beast she had hoped the Animal Control had picked up and impounded.

"Down, Brutus."

At the quiet command of his master, the dog crouched at his feet and raised the shaggy face toward her. If there were eyes behind that shag, they seemed to be asking for her sympathy. Well, in a way, the monster had her sympathy all right. They both had the same master!

"What do you want?" Veronica asked.

Holman Devonshire studied her face for a moment. "The blue is good on you," he decided.

Nobody needed to tell her that blue was her color. But, "I was about to take it off!" she said.

The strange eyes lighted up with interest. And Veronica felt herself blush and hated herself for it. "That wasn't what I meant—I—I—"

Well, there she was being clumsy again. How could this man manage to bring out the worst in her at every meeting? But her husband's eyes no longer held any light. They were hard and cold. She had probably imagined the interest anyway. Lately, she was having trouble sorting fact from fantasy in her strange, new world.

"I came to tell you that my lawyer will be moving in today and has suggested that you and I do the long-delayed inventory. I would like you to cancel any tours you've scheduled—"

"That's impossible."

"Impossible, my dear? I thought *nothing* was impossible with God."

"Stop it. Stop it this minute!" Veronica was close

to tears. "I won't have you poking fun at my faith—at me—at us—"

To her disgust her voice gave way to the lump in her throat.

"I'm sorry. I truly am." Holman moved as if to touch Veronica and quickly she drew back. He shrugged then. "I was about to say that basically I agree with you—oh, what's the use!"

For a moment the man had seemed to be sincere. But she must be on guard for that kind of deceptive behavior. "We can do the inventory some other time—" she began.

"We will do it today!"

With that, he reached for the doorknob as if to close the door on matters. Then he paused. "Your dress will be here today—the one for the party. It's gold."

"I don't like gold. Silver is more—"

"The dress is gold," he repeated. "And tomorrow night you will be my golden goddess—a part of our bargain, you know. Heel, Brutus!"

On command the great dog pulled his shaggy body upright to stand beside his master's knee. When Holman Devonshire turned, the dog, still almost touching the man's leg, turned with him. Together, man and dog moved down the long, shadowy hall. Fascinated, Veronica watched the dog's hind parts wobble beneath his weight, his blunt, tailless shape keeping step with the man beside him.

Heel, Brutus! Heel, Veronica! Heel heart. She turned from the door with a dry sob. "That's not right," she whispered brokenly. "It's *healing,* I need Lord. Heal this bitterness in my heart!" Veronica sank down beside her canopied bed and poured out her heart in prayer as she had not been able to do for a long time. And at length peace came.

The inventory took all day. Veronica was relieved that her husband brought a secretary with him. He scarcely

introduced the spinsterlike woman, simply calling her
"Miss Hoffman." The other woman's presence speeded
up the listing as the three of them moved from room to
room past eighteenth-century porcelains, inlaid woods—
each shading into another—mother-of-pearl, gold leaf, and
hand-painted vases . . . all of it representing the life of
careful buying by Hugh Rosemead and the generations
before him.

Veronica was grateful, too, for Miss Hoffman's presence
because she did not wish to be alone with Holman Devonshire. He remained in the background as she gave quick
identifications to pieces especially dear to her heart, raising no protest when she explained that they were among
the most precious of the Rosemead collection.

At several points, Veronica paused and made notes of
her own. "This is where the gold cross will be when it
is returned," she said meaningfully.

Then, when she discovered that other valuable items
were missing, she made no comment. After all, why
arouse the suspicions of the secretary? She would take the
matter up with the culprit in private. There could be no
doubt that the man she had married was a gambler, a thief,
and more! Oh, why hadn't she consented to his suggestion that they do the inventory immediately?

In her frustration, it did not occur to Veronica that it
was she who had postponed the matter. She only knew a
deep sadness at the disappearance of the collections. Well,
there was always her looked-forward-to "someday." Holman
Devonshire would make a fatal slip and she would be
there watching. She could drop this act she was putting
on for everyone, including herself, and be the undisputed
mistress of her father's property. Some day. . . .

The dress arrived in the late afternoon, but there
was no time to try it on. Veronica put the great box
with the exotic wrapping and ribbons away in her
closet and was about to rest for a few minutes before

dressing for dinner when she heard a commotion downstairs. At first, there were only voices. Then, came the sound of something large and heavy being pushed across the floor. Her first thought was of the time-polished floors and the roped-off area, carpeted with old but priceless Persian rugs. Surely nobody would shove heavy objects across the sections. James had a dolly...and who could be making such a racket anyway?

Then she heard Hilda's voice, loud and shrill, protesting—only she was unable to make out the words. Finally, when she heard a male voice, unrecognizable in its high pitch, call out for help, she wondered what on earth could be so heavy.

But the call for help had not been because of the objects being moved, Veronica learned as she opened her bedroom door a crack. What she saw was startling. Thurman Shield, hand drawn protectively up in front of his face, was trying to crouch in back of one of the heavy crates he was directing the movers to load onto the waiting dolly and wheel into her father's study. And between Veronica and the scene below stood Brutus, every hair on his great body bristled to double his size. Looking ready to pounce with the slightest movement of his victims, the dog was guarding the stairway leading first to her room then to her father's offices.

Was the dog vicious? She didn't know. Certainly, he looked it and there was not time to decide.

"Down, Brutus!" Veronica tried to make her voice as calm as her husband's when he spoke to the animal, even though her heart was pounding with fear.

More to her surprise than anybody else's apparently, the dog crouched obediently. She hurried down the curving stairs, not sure what he would do next. In the seconds it took her to descend, the animal did

not move. Neither did he turn his shaggy head from the
men who stood like statues. He would hold them at bay.
No doubt about it.

"It's all right, Brutus," Veronica said. "Mr. Shield will
be staying here."

The great dog turned a shaggy face toward her and
whined as if asking for something. Praise? She couldn't
bring herself to touch this creature, could she? She'd taken
a giant step forward (or backward!) to address this beast.
I've never spoken to a dog before in my life, she thought, *but
to touch one? It's unthinkable. . . .*

In the split second of indecision, Veronica felt rather
than saw eyes on her. Brutus's eyes, if indeed he had any,
were glued to his captives. Raising her gaze only slightly,
she saw that Holman Devonshire had entered the great
reception room from the east wing. His eyes were watching. Waiting. *Testing.*

But, of course! She was his bought-and-paid-for hostess.
And, for all practical purposes, the mistress of the Castle
Loma. Her duties undoubtedly included being in control
of household pets.

Returning her eyes to Thurman Shield and the movers,
Veronica squared her shoulders and forced a smile.
She was caught at a disadvantage as usual, but something
happened in that moment. Her natural dignity returned.
From now on, she knew that she could play the part
well.

"Good boy," she said gently to the dog at her feet. The
great beast lifted a grateful head and to her amazement
managed to nose his face beneath her upraised hand.
Veronica stroked the head and as the hair parted she had
a first glimpse of a pair of great gray-green eyes beneath
it. Why, the dog adored her! Involuntarily, her head went
up and her eyes locked with her husband's again. She
knew that the day had been too taxing when she imagined
that she saw a flicker of the same expression Brutus wore.

Tearing her gaze away, Veronica walked quickly to greet Thurman Shield. Extending both hands, "Welcome to Castle Loma," she said.

He took her hands warmly and his voice, when he spoke, was grateful. "Thank you, Veronica. Oh, it was good to see you!"

Holman Devonshire seemed to have covered the distance between them all in one giant stride. "Well now!" he said. "I was unaware that you two were on such familiar terms. That simplifies matters a lot!"

It didn't, of course. It complicated *everything*. . . .

• • •

June twenty-first. Her birthday! Veronica awoke with a headache. Small wonder after yesterday's excitement. The strain of the inventory. The awkwardness of Thurman's arrival. Her learning that he was to be "one of the family" and would be appearing each evening for dinner which would serve to draw out the charade to even greater lengths. Then, pleading the headache which waited until this morning to develop, she had escaped to her room only to find another surprising and somehow disturbing turn of events. There on her dressing table had lain the copy of her inventory, which she was required to sign before it was placed in the vault, and something more! An inventory of the entire household—even the missing pieces from her father's collections.

From the depths of her soft bed, Veronica heard the rustle of clothing. Hilda? But what was Hilda doing up before daylight? She stopped massaging her temples and dared to open her eyes. In the dim light of a carefully-shaded lamp Hilda was smoothing the folds of something which seemed to shimmer with light.

Her dress. The one her husband had ordered from Miami. And had ordered her to wear.

From downstairs came the sound of running water, a muted rattle of dishes, and the swish-swish of water from the sprinklers against the lawns, hedges, and flower beds. And here in the bedroom, Hilda—unaware that she was being watched—was preparing "Miss Veronica's golden gown" and softly humming, "Happy birthday!"

Yesterday's humidity seemed to have given way to a whisper of the trade winds. It would be a beautiful day everywhere except where it mattered. In her heart.

When she stirred, Hilda asked softly, "Are you awake, Miss Veronica?"

"Yes, Hilda, but I have a terrible headache."

"I'll get you some aspirin."

Hilda started toward the door but stopped suddenly when there came a distinct sound of footsteps from the attic followed by a dull, continuous sound as if something heavy were being dragged across the uncarpeted floor. *I've heard that noise before,* Veronica thought, *but who and what is it?*

Suddenly, in spite of her aching head, Veronica sat bolt upright in bed. It occurred to her that she had forgotten about the collector's items in the attic in yesterday's inventory. Worse, she had no idea of what all of them were. Her father's most recent buys from Europe and China were never uncrated. He had fallen ill before work on the new wing could take place. Then Veronica had learned that there was no money remaining, that the old mansion itself was heavily mortgaged, and that the dream—like her father—must die. . . .

"Hilda, have you any idea what's up there?" Veronica tried to tilt her head toward the attic, but the pain in her head increased.

The older woman noticed her discomfort. "Lie down,

child," she begged, trying to plump Veronica's pillow for greater comfort.

But Veronica waved her away. "*Do* you, Hilda?"

Hilda sat down on the edge of the bed. "No," she said slowly as if trying to recall, "not exactly. I did hear Mr. Rosemead tell your mother about some Meissen porcelain and all the antiques from the castle in Spain, the *big* one, and all its fine linens and silver. Mrs. Rosemead loved the silver, you know, more than she likes some of the things—"

Hilda's voice trailed off when the sounds from the attic were repeated. "I hear it lots, Miss Veronica. And talk is—" Again the housekeeper checked herself. "I'll get the aspirin."

"Wait, Hilda! What were you going to say?"

Dawn was streaking the sky. In the pale light, Hilda's face showed signs of strain. Veronica wondered if it was due to an overload of work the party had brought on or if something was troubling her. Something she preferred or dared not discuss.

"Hilda, you know you can trust me," she encouraged.

Nervously, Hilda pushed at a loose hairpin and secured it before she spoke. "Oh, it's not that! It's just that I don't like speaking against the dead—"

"The *dead?*" Veronica's voice was almost a whisper. "My father?"

"Well, it's only talk and I try to stamp it out!" Hilda's voice rose in anger then she lowered it again to add, "But there are those who claim some of the things are ill-gotten gains—that he was somehow involved in—well—"

When the older woman hesitated, Veronica whispered, "Go on."

"Well, maybe smuggling—or that some of the things are forgeries—gossip, of course. Evil gossip. Your father was a God-fearing man unless—"

Hilda gave a gasp as if horrified at what she was about to say. Then something in Veronica's stricken face must have prompted her to continue. "Even if I believed a word of it, I know it was to pay Mr. Gilbert's debts and Mrs. Rosemead's doctor bills—of course, it's not true! Now, don't go worrying your pretty head on your birthday. And speaking of your head—"

Hilda rose from her tense perch on the edge of the bed as if eager to be off on an errand. But Veronica detained her.

"But what has this to do with the noises we heard?" she asked in a desperate voice.

"I don't know. I simply don't know. And, frankly, me and my James thought it best we not meddle. Something's going on for sure, but frankly I have been afraid to investigate." Her face lighted up then. "But now that Count Devonshire's here, we have nothing to worry about. Maybe I should have James tell him what we heard—"

"No!" Veronica was surprised at the feeling she had put into the word. When she saw Hilda's puzzled face, she was forced to add, "I mean, let me do it—and not today, Hilda."

"Of course not today, Miss Veronica," Hilda soothed. She left then for the aspirin and when she returned with it she also brought an enormous armful of crimson sweetheart roses, 25 of them. "One for each year of your beautiful life," the card said and it was signed, "With love, your husband."

It was a busy day. And yet the hands on the clock seemed to crawl. Probably because Veronica wanted it over and done with so badly. Her headache worsened, but there was no time to lie down. She had to rely on black coffee and too much aspirin instead, a combination which left her feeling weak and with a gnawing in her stomach. She did not go down for dinner, having Hilda explain her absence, and it was with an effort that she showered and slipped into some of the silk-soft lingerie purchased on her honeymoon.

As she dusted her body with talc, a feeling of euphoria began to spread over her being. The whole world was unreal. She wasn't sure she liked the feeling of being out of control. But, on the other hand she decided, it took the edge off her nerves and made her incapable of feeling as deeply the sense of depression, apprehension, and fear that had plagued her during the last three days.

A maid in a black dress and white frilly apron, hired for the evening, brought up a small package, curtsied and disappeared. Usually, gifts waited until the "witching hour," as her father called it—midnight of the family member's birthday—so the sender had to be an outsider.

Quickly, she tore open the tissue wrapping. Inside was a small but obviously expensive bottle of imported perfume. "I would be honored to have you wear a drop of this *parfum de violette* this evening," the note inside read. It was signed "Thurman."

It was a lovely gesture. But the thought of perfume made her sick. Some other time maybe. Now, she must hurry. There was her hair to do and it gave every indication of being even more uncontrollable than usual.

Since her every wish was being granted except for the one nobody knew about, Veronica felt less surprised than she normally would have when a hairdresser arrived. The petite blonde as unable to speak English, so Veronica allowed the girl to fuss with her long, fine hair, make clucking noises, and at last give an exaggerated exclamation of satisfaction.

When the dress had arrived yesterday, Veronica had considered returning it to the shop unopened. No, she couldn't cause a scene. That was forbidden by contract. Instead, she had decided to wear the hateful black dress she was married in. That should do Holman Devonshire in....

But tonight she felt too lethargic to fight the man. Instead, she pulled the long, close-fitting—but not suggestively so—gold dress over her head, being careful not to disturb her hair. The effect was startling. The reflection staring back at her could not be Veronica Rosemead. No, of course not! It was the Contiesse de Devonshire. Dressed for the kill.

Just before descending the wide stairway, Veronica lingered in the shadows of a potted palm on the landing, hoping that the moment would prepare her for the glittering crowds. It didn't, of course. It only served to unnerve her. *How, oh how, am I going to get through this evening—no, night—didn't Hilda say there is to be a buffet at ten, followed by midnight dinner and breakfast in the wee hours?* Quickly—knowing she might be detected at any moment—her eyes searched for Eleanore Rosemead. *I should have checked on Mother,* she thought with guilt—*her clothes, her hair, the things that are important to her.* Then, with relief, Veronica spotted her and gasped.

Her mother, so recently the grieving widow, was seated on a white brocade couch. Having changed her mode of dress from black chiffon to white piped in black as the weeks wore on, Eleanore Rosemead now wore stark white. Around her slender throat was a band of emeralds, a gift from her late husband. Veronica remembered that he had refused to pawn them for even a few days when the first real financial crisis came, preferring to mortgage the Castle Loma instead. One would think the jewels would be precious to its owner. But her mother had never worn the necklace again until tonight. It was all so mystifying. Life before her father's death. And life afterward. Somehow it had to all fit together. But *how?* She was on a roller coaster in Disney World. Up and down. . . up and down. . . up and down. No it was a merry-go-round. Roller coasters had a destination. But her world simply went round and round. . . .

At the dizzying thought, Veronica felt herself sway. She reached for the support of the polished banister, leaning just enough to touch it. The slight movement lowered her view. *Why, Mother had no robe over her lap,* she thought in dismay. Well, maybe one good thing had come of this make-believe marriage. Dr. Gillian said that Mother needed "total confidence." She seemed to have it. Right now, she was surrounded by sophisticated people who seemed captivated by her charms. From force of habit Veronica waited for her mother to complete her sentence, draw a polite laugh, and lower her slender, gesturing hand before taking the first step down the long, red-carpeted stairs.

Later, Veronica was never able to put a coherent memory of the party together. Like the fragments of a dream, nothing stayed in place. There was a myriad of faces in a parade of women in fashionable gowns and men in black ties. . . all of them holding slender-stemmed glasses and talking in brittle voices of places she had never been. *Not that they know,* she recalled thinking. *They expect me to be sophisticated and widely-traveled and so their eyes see what they expect to see.* Her natural reserve gave her dignity—"statuesque," one newspaper described her. And her ability to respond to questions regarding the furnishings gave her needed confidence. "Yes, neo-rococo. . . 1851, to be exact. . . no, this one is older, Frankenthal, 1755. . . the porcelain clock? Angelica did it in Paris. . . ."

Somewhere in the glittering crowd was Gilbert. Veronica did not see him. She simply knew he was there by the tingling of her scalp. Gilbert's presence meant trouble. "Oh, dear Lord, get me through the evening. Get us *all* through it—somehow." Over and over she prayed the prayer.

Only one thing stood out in her mind. Holman Devonshire, who met her at the bottom of the stairs with a convincing look of open adoration on his face, never left her side. His steadying hand was ever at her elbow. His words of false endearment were ever in her ear. But there was no choice. She must lean on him. For his audience, yes. But for support as well. Otherwise, she might crumple at any given moment. Then, this whole tinseled evening, whatever its purpose, would shatter like the cheap bauble it was.

When the buffet was announced, he steered her to the table well ahead of the guests. There, to her total surpise, was a beautifully-appointed table centered by a nosegay of violets and surrounded by crystal and china—for *tea!* No champagne and caviar. No fancy finger foods. Bracing amber tea . . . smoked salmon and watercress . . . scones with whipped cream and jams . . . Dundee cakes, custard tarts, and what looked suspiciously like lemon curd.

Veronica looked questioningly at her husband's face. Was this his idea of a cruel joke? But the incredibly handsome face showed no sign of mockery. The gold-flecked eyes for one disconcerting moment looked like those of a child who is eager to please.

"Do you like it?" he asked.

"I do, but I don't understand."

Holman Devonshire gave her hand a squeeze of open affection for the benefit of eyes which were beginning to turn toward them. Without warning, he leaned down to brush a curl on her forehead with a light kiss. Then, just as quickly, he lifted his head to address his guests.

"The cocktail hour has officially ended," he announced. "Those seeking watering holes will have to sojourn to the Sea Oats. Right, Rhoda?"

There was a polite ripple of laughter and a few jesting remarks, but Veronica heard none of them. Rhoda! Rhoda Tucker was *here?* How dare this man! He knew what the girl was to her brother and any other man who cared to take a room at the inn. *Maybe himself included,* she thought hotly.

Veronica recovered quickly. If he chose to turn this into a Boston Tea Party, it was no concern of hers. Secretly, she was highly pleased. But she was puzzled. And she did not like the strange galaxy of emotions that he evoked. Her job would be easier if he would stay in character. Not that she was going to be taken in—and having Rhoda Tucker here could wait until—

A familiar voice broke into her thoughts, syllables of the words slurred by alcohol. "Person—sonally th' bride's li'l brother-er pre—prefers bourbon 'n wa-er."

"Lower your voice or I'll drag you out of here!" Her husband's voice was low but it carried the same command he used on Brutus. "You will drink tea or nothing. *Now!*"

Avoiding the eyes of persons who might have overheard, Veronica looked down to where the bosom of her gold cloth gown pulsed up and down from her heavy heartbeat. Holman Devonshire's eyes followed hers. "It's all right," he whispered.

Veronica dared to glance up and to her surprise it was as he said. Her brother had accepted a cup of hot tea and slunk away. Of course, the evening was young. But she breathed a little prayer of thanksgiving that they had finished Act I.

Someone forced a dainty sandwich into her hand and Holman Devonshire urged her to eat. "Fortify yourself, Veronica. There is apt to be a lot of action."

She glanced quickly at him to see just what the comment meant. But his eyes were averted as he poured her a cup of tea.

When food was on their plates, her husband suggested that they move onto the veranda. Oh, she would welcome fresh air, but what about the others?

He shrugged. The guests wouldn't miss them. Her brother he would keep an eye on. And, he explained, "I talked your mother into resting for a time in order to be up for the fireworks at midnight. Isn't that when you receive your gifts?"

Veronica gave him a look of appreciation and was rewarded by a rare smile. But the moment was broken by a willowy redhead with a lazy smile who laid a familiar hand on his arm. "How very *British* of you—this tea, and such a grand party."

When he would have moved away, she detained him to inquire of persons Veronica did not know. As she waited for him to terminate the conversation, there were voices from behind the wine-and-gold drapes which separated the receiving room from the conservatory.

"How did she do it?"

"The money, of course."

"Now, be fair, darling," the first woman's voice said in mock-pleading. "The man has everything. A title. And he's handsome, dashing, and devoted—"

"Devoted to money, you mean!" the first voice interrupted in a stage-whisper. "And doesn't care how he accumulates it. The contiesse—some distinction—" the woman mocked, "wouldn't be the first American to swap a fortune for a title!"

Veronica whirled around to see who the speakers were. But her husband's hand was on her arm and she was forced to walk the short distance to the doors opening onto the wide veranda.

Fortunately, it was deserted. Holman Devonshire pulled out a wrought-iron chair and none too soon. Veronica sank into it gratefully, sure that her legs would not have supported her another split second.

"It's a beautiful night for the party. Full moon and all the makings." His voice was low and pleasant.

But Veronica did not notice the tone. Neither did she appreciate the heady odor of magnolias mingled with heliotrope or the soft, contented twitter of the birds that nested in the cypress trees.

She forced herself to take a tiny bite of the sandwich on her plate before answering. And then her words had nothing to do with the beauty of the night around them.

"You heard. You know what they're saying."

"I don't *care* what they say—except for your sake."

"And these women, they know you—well, don't they?" Her voice was so flat that it sounded unfamiliar to her ears.

"Veronica, they don't matter—"

"They *do* matter. And what's more, that barmaid you brought—" How dare he laugh!

" 'Barmaid' is no longer the phrase. Rhoda is a cocktail waitress."

"Among other things—and she's not welcome in my— this house."

She heard him inhale. "I had my reasons for having her here. And you are to be gracious to any guest I welcome here. Already you are in danger of breaking the terms of your contract. One violation—" He laughed again. And his voice trailed away as he strode inside. She was alone for the first time.

It was good to lift her aching head and let the light breeze finger with her hair and cool her hot cheeks. The tea and sandwich had strengthened her a bit, but a feeling of unreality lingered. Below her the smoothly-manicured lawns sloped gently to the cliffs above the sea. Moonlight bathed the formal hedges, all disciplined by last-minute shearing to perfect shapes. The taller hedges of hibiscus flanked by bamboo were allowed to retain their natural shapes to form a pleasing foil. The east garden was dark except for the night-lights which filtered through the heather and ferns, but the rose gardens to the west were illuminated with countless colored lanterns, their light picking up each detail then reflecting on the white-capped waves of the ocean below. It was spectacular. But too elaborate. Too false. Too—something Veronica could not express with words. She wished the golden gown were back on its gray satin hanger and that she wore something long, filmy, and white and could wander barefoot in her own Secret Garden of flowers. A slight smile curved her lips at the thought of what the society pages would do with *that.*

"Smell the heliotrope?"

Veronica jumped when a male voice she recognized spoke to her out of the darkness. "Thurman!" she said in , surprise.

Those people are like that—the heliotrope, I mean."

There seemed to be so much the two of them should discuss. Certainly, it was not heliotrope. But the idea intrigued her so she asked him why the comparison.

"Low brilliance," he explained. "And following the sun."

Was he speaking of himself? Veronica wondered again what a man like Thurman Shield was doing here in the village. Once perhaps, had their friendship bloomed as she would have liked, she would have felt no hesitancy in drawing him out. Now, there was an invisible wall between them. Remembering, she felt herself stiffen as she wondered what she should say now that they were alone together for the first time since her marriage.

It was Thurman who spoke. "I want you to know," he began uncertainly and then he spoke rapidly as if he expected to be interrupted before saying what was on his mind, "that I had no idea when Holman asked me to prepare the papers that the—the other party was you. He gave no name at first. And somehow he did not meet my expectations." He did not say how and Veronica did not ask.

"I understand," she said quietly, wondering if she did.

"And as to my presence here—have you wondered why I accepted the offer to become his personal attorney?"

"I have wondered about so many things—" she said vaguely and then caught herself. After all, this was Holman Devonshire's attorney. And she was Holman Devonshire's wife.

Thurman took a step toward where Veronica stood. "Are you happy, Veronica?"

The question, asked in a low, concerned voice took Veronica completely by surprise. "I—I—" she began helplessly, "I don't know."

"You don't have to pretend with me, Veronica." Thurman leaned forward. The movement was more in order that they could talk without being overheard than an attempt at intimacy. Even so, Veronica felt herself draw back instinctively. It would endanger her position to reveal too much. Besides, she wasn't sure she knew at the moment exactly what her feelings were. Life was so confusing. . . .

Thurman's face was just inches from hers. "Go on, tell me how things are," he urged gently.

Looking up at him then, Veronica saw the concern in his eyes. They were a deeper gray than she had imagined and he did not have on the horn-rimmed glasses. And their depth was greater as if she could drown in them. Peacefully. Away from this runaway world that lacked the purpose she needed.

"I feel," she said through numb lips, "exactly the way I felt when I was a little girl and banged my head against the door jamb. Dazed—out of control—''

Their gazes held. The lanterns in the rose garden swayed with the night breeze to pick up the silver lights in his hair. ''You must either be in control or be controlled. Act or react,'' he said.

''None of us are in control completely.''

''Maybe not in all matters, but in this marriage—''

''Please,'' she whispered. ''We shouldn't be discussing my marriage—''

''Shouldn't be, but you are!''

Only one man in the world had a rich, deep voice like that. ''Holman—'' Veronica, unaware that she had used her husband's name for the first time, swayed toward him.

Reaching out to encircle her waist, Holman Devonshire righted her position. ''Come, my dear, we must be getting back to your party,'' he said as if gently chiding a child.

The world had stopped. Her heart had stopped. Only the soft tendrils of Veronica's hair, which always seemed to be in perpetual motion, dared stir. Without being conscious of moving, she allowed herself to be escorted back into the sea of plastic faces. The lift she had felt from the tea and sandwich was gone and the euphoria took over again.

Sometime later, time having lost its meaning, Veronica excused herself to go to the powder room. *Anything,* she thought wildly, *to escape, and I dare not go outdoors again. That was a close call, providing I got through it.*

At first, she thought the mirrored rooms were deserted, but before she could appreciate the thought there was a crisp whisper of taffeta. A woman's figure emerged from the shadows of the sitting room.

''Sorry, ma'am—contiesse,'' she corrected quickily.

One of the maids her husband had engaged for the

evening? Not likely dressed in a tight-fitting red dress and matching ankle-strap shoes. Veronica felt an unexplainable surge of pity for the young woman. The obviously cheap clothes were all wrong as was the heavy mask of makeup and the Shirley-Temple curls.

"Is there something I can do for you?" Veronica asked kindly.

"Oh, no, Your Highness! You have done far too much already—letting me come here to see this grand place—"

The voice, though lacking the modulation that comes from good breeding, was low and pleasant. But the color-less eyes were wide with fear. Veronica's eyes took in the low-cut dress, the ringed fingers, and somehow knew before she asked. "Are you Rhoda Tucker—from the Sea Oats?"

She seemed to cower as if fearing she would be struck. "I shouldn't have come," she whispered.

"You were invited. Of course, you should have come," Veronica said as cordially as she was able. Inside, anger flared in her heart. How could her husband be so cruel as to expose this person, no matter what she was, to his jet-set friends? As if there wouldn't be gossip enough about this evening!

"But the invitation should've come from you, ma'am—Your Highness—"

Veronica's pity deepened. "Just Mrs. Devonshire." The name sounded strange and she hesitated before continuing. When Rhoda nodded her appreciation, Veronica said, "It was my husband who mailed out the invitations."

The colorless eyes opened even wider. "But I didn't get no invitation, ma'am. Mr. Gilbert just asked me."

"My brother?"

"The same. Said I could be a big help, he did. And get to see how rich folks act, too. But I don't see how much help I've been—him disappearing and all—''

Panic seized Veronica's heart. The shock of Rhoda's presence and the fact that it was Gilbert instead of Holman Devonshire who was responsible was enough to add another layer to her already fogged-over brain. And now this!

"When did you last see him?" Veronica forced her voice to sound calm. She did not wish to arouse any more suspicions than necessary.

"Right after His Highness—Count Devonshire—put a stop to the drinkin'. Said there was some business needin' his care. He went upstairs."

"Perhaps to his room," Veronica said uncertainly, sure that the conclusion was wrong. "How long have you been here, Rhoda?"

" 'Bout an hour, ma'am. I—I didn't know where to wait."

And nobody bothered to show you, poor girl, Veronica thought in shame. She reached out and took one of the plump hands. "Would you like to go home?"

"Oh, yes, ma'am!" The girl's eagerness was pathetic.

"I will have James take you."

"Oh, thank you, thank you, Mrs. Devonshire, ma'am! And I promise I won't say nothin' about anything—even when people ask."

Veronica felt a thrill of fear along her spine. "Are there people who ask questions about us, Rhoda?"

"Oh, yes'm, but me, I know better now. You're nice— real nice. Like this man today who claimed he was a peace officer askin' how to get up Enchanted Hill. I told 'im he'd have to follow his nose," she giggled, "and if he made it, I'd see 'im here. But then he said no, he'd be hidin' in the bushes!"

"Probably he is a watchman," Veronica said guardedly, believing no such thing.

"I don't think so, ma'am," Rhoda said doubtfully,

"but then, like I say, I don't answer questions, so I don't ask 'em."

"That is wise," Veronica smiled as the two of them prepared to leave.

Rhoda beamed at the word of approval. "Thank you, ma'am, and if ever I can be of any help—"

"I will remember that." Then, on impulse as they left by a side door leading onto a private terrace, Veronica asked, "Would you wish to attend one of the Sunday worship services we have here—that is, when we resume them?"

The girl hesitated. "You mean like *church*?"

Veronica smiled. "Somewhat. There is no sermon, however, except on the few occasions that Reverend Crussell has been able to meet with us. We read the Bible, have prayer, and sing hymns."

"I can sing real nice," Rhoda Tucker said shyly. "Yes, I'd like to come sometime if it's no trouble. Nobody ever asked me to church before."

When James appeared with the car, Veronica waved good-bye and hurried up the back stairway. She should be getting back to the party. Her husband would be looking for her and she was unable to handle any more emotional upsets than the evening had afforded already. But it was imperative that she check Gilbert's room for his whereabouts. But he was not there, of course.

Neither did she see him the rest of the night, which passed like a terrible nightmare. Veronica remembered only bits and pieces, none of it fitting together. Dinner was elaborate, but she could not recall the menu. There were gifts, but she could remember none of them except for a plain white envelope which bore her name and her husband's signature below it, but she had no recollection of what she did with it. Then there were fireworks that seemed to go on forever...

each wildly beautiful at first then inevitably explod-
ing with deafening noise followed by an even louder
silence. Like her head. Like the evening. Like her
life...trouble lay ahead...if not tonight...soon, *very*
soon....

Finally when she could bear no more, Veronica sought
out her husband who seemed engrossed in serious conversation with two men she had not met during the evening. Laying a hand on his arm, she whispered, "I can't
bear any more—"

If his concern were not real, Holman Devonshire
put on a good show. "I will have Hilda see you to your
room," he decided after one quick look at her drawn,
white face.

"But the guests—my responsibility—"

"I will handle things. Then we will talk tomorrow."

Tomorrow—oh, blessed tomorrow—when this dreadful
charade was behind her. Tomorrow would be a day of
recovery. And somehow, difficult though it had been, the
Lord had seen fit to answer her prayer. He had held her
up throughout.

Veronica fell down across her bed, fully clothed and
too exhausted to care. Only once did she lift her head
and that was to let the little breeze caress her face.
The lights were out, she saw. And then her tired eyes
caught sight of something else. Silhouetted against
the moon which had now dropped toward the western
horizon, there was the distinct outline of a large boat. No,
it was larger than a boat, more of a ship. It was moving,
she decided, but why without lights? Then her tired mind
could think no more.

She dropped into a troubled sleep dreaming that
she stood in the midst of her mint bed with Brutus
beside her. Gilbert appeared, begging for protection
which she felt too weak to offer. But when Thurman
came for her brother, he gave up trying to drag Gilbert

from the spot because of his fear of Brutus. Holman Devonshire controlled the dog, but the mint bed made him sneeze. The struggle went on for hours with Veronica wanting to escape but not knowing which man to go with . . . and besides she could not leave Gilbert alone . . . .

Chapter 7

The tomorrow her husband had promised as a time when they would talk was a long time in coming. When Veronica went down to breakfast the following morning Hilda said that he had been called away on business. When? Shortly after she retired. The guests? Oh, most of them grew bored when His Highness stood by his announcement that there would be no more drinks. And stick by it, he did—even locked the cellar door—

Veronica set down the pitcher from which she was pouring chilled orange juice. "Why is the door locked, Hilda? There is no wine there and hasn't been since Gilbert took to drinking heavily. Where *is* my brother, by the way?"

Hilda didn't know, she said. The woman seemed flustered at the question, causing Veronica to suspect that Mother had cautioned her against talking about Gilbert, so she inquired about her mother instead.

Hilda's face lighted up. "Oh, Mrs. Rosemead is

fine. Sleeping like a lamb. I haven't seen her so happy since—well, the accident."

Veronica set her orange juice glass down with planned deliberation. Then she poured herself a cup of coffee and walked to the open glass doors that overlooked the greenhouse and citrus grove before speaking. With her back to Hilda, she asked softly, "What do you know of the accident, Hilda? I've never asked you before."

She heard Hilda inhale sharply. "Nothing, Miss Veronica! We know nothing—James and me!"

But she had hesitated too long before speaking. Somebody had silenced her. Veronica spun around with a suddenness that caught the housekeeper off guard. "Has my mother coached you?"

"Oh, no—nothing like that!" The woman was wringing her hands.

"Don't be afraid to answer me, Hilda. Nothing is going to happen to you. I will see to that personally. But I must find some answers. There are things in my own life which I must settle and I can't settle them without some help."

When there was no answer, Veronica asked, "Has my husband—"

"Oh no!" There was a ring of desperation in Hilda's voice and a haunted look in her face. "He's a good man no matter what your father thought. Why, just this morning he ordered all that leftover food sent to the poor down in the slums section back of the new casino—"

"I know where it is, Hilda, and that was a noble gesture," Veronica interrupted. Admittedly, her husband was a constant surprise. However, she wasn't going to be taken in by one of his better moods. "But we were talking about the accident, Hilda," she said.

Hilda's agitation gave way to a determined silence.

"James and me, we're loyal to this family we work for."

Veronica took the woman's work-reddened hand in hers. "I know. How well I know. And I love you for that. But, Hilda, in a very real sense, you work for a new family now and I am a part of it."

"But he—"

"*He,* Hilda? My husband? Gilbert—or James?"

"Oh, no! Miss Veronica!" Hilda's agitation had returned. "Mr.—" Then, as if she had committed a grave wrong, she jerked free of Veronica and covered her face with shaking hands.

"My father." Veronica spoke the words in awe, more to herself than to the woman in front of her. Then a great question loomed in her mind—one which had never occurred to her. Was her father shielding someone else or was he protecting his own image? He was a proud man. A righteous man. But one who did not want his ideas challenged or the family name tainted. Might he have been tempted—

And then she put the idea away as unworthy. How could she, the daughter who idolized her father, doubt him? Especially now that he was gone and not here to defend himself. Whatever he had said or done was right and proper. And she would see to it that his memory was respected—and his every wish carried out!

Neither her brother nor her husband showed up during the morning. Veronica was glad that it was Sunday, a day which she tried to keep as free as possible, unless there were unusual circumstances. She needed the day of rest, particularly today. However, tomorrow was overcrowded, the number of tourists having increased to the point that she was going to need help, so today she must attend to some matters of vital importance in spite of her fatigue.

First, her devotional. She needed a talk with the Lord as much as she needed a rest. But it was obvious that she was going to get neither. When she tried to read her Bible, the words ran together and her mind refused to shut out the problems at hand.

"I hope You will understand, Lord, and forgive me if what I am about to do is wrong." With that broken little prayer, Veronica laid her Bible aside and slipped quietly down the hall leading to the attic stairs. Mother was sleeping. Hilda would think she herself was resting. Both Gil and Holman Devonshire were gone. What better time to try to put an end to some of the mysteries going on at the Castle Loma?

The attic was dark, larger than she remembered, but lower-beamed. It was often necessary to bend forward to protect her head as she moved between the packing boxes and pieces of furniture draped in sheets to protect their surfaces from scratches and dust. There was a bare bulb hanging from the center of the room, but before turning it on, Veronica cautiously closed the drapes on the two small windows. The light was inadequate, but at least it would keep her from stumbling. Inching her way back to where she had stood a few moments before in the center of the room, Veronica had the uncanny feeling that someone else was in the room with her. When there was no sound, she dismissed the idea as foolish. Moments later she decided that the idea came from footprints, obviously those of a man's shoes, which showed in the heavy layer of dust on the floor alongside her own. On close examination, she saw that the sizes were different. Two sets of footprints! No, it was three! Some of them more recent than others. Whose were they and why were the men here?

A thrill of fear rippled along her spine. Maybe it would be wise to leave things as they were...no, whatever was going on was something she had to know. Otherwise, she was going to become paranoid. Not knowing who were friends, she would think all of them to be her enemies—that there was a conspiracy to destroy herself and her family. But *why*? Maybe solution to one question would lead to answers for the others. So thinking, she turned to the crates.

Some of the crates had been opened. She would examine those first. But when she would have reached into the nearest box, it was empty except for excelsior in which her father's art objects had been packed. It was true then. Somebody was taking the valuable pieces from the attic. Holman Devonshire, of course. But, even though she had no doubt that the man was capable of doing whatever suited his ends, a question rose in her mind. Why should he when the property was his anyway? Unless, of course, it was to pay his gambling debts or to pay for such posh parties as last night's. With her dead father's money! Her face tightened. There was an uncomfortable knotting in her stomach muscles. And something surprising and sickening happened to her heart. For suddenly Veronica realized the awful truth. She had hoped, a secret hidden even from herself, that Holman Devonshire was not involved.

But there was no future with this man. She knew that. He had made it perfectly clear that he was everything her father said of him and that he had no intention of changing. There was no hope or happiness ahead...and, besides, there was her responsibility to her father. With renewed resolve to do whatever needed to be done to be rid of this violent man and to free her family, Veronica returned to the job at hand.

But the other crates were empty too, except perhaps for the few stacked one on top of the other in the far corner of the attic. Wondering how she could reach the top box, pry off the lid, and investigate the contents by herself, she moved several of the empty crates to the corner and tried to arrange them into steps. The arrangement was poor at best. The steps were too far between and the crates were flimsy, their tops uneven.

When at last she managed to pull herself to the top, the crates swayed crazily and more than once Veronica thought they would collapse beneath her weight. Hanging onto the opened crates for support, she managed to pry off the lid of the top crate piece by piece, conscious of tearing the flesh of her hands, breaking her nails, and bruising her arms. Still she was driven to claw at the splintering wood until she was able to reach into the opening and draw out the first piece. It felt like a heavy urn, possibly metal, and it was wrapped in yellowing newspapers.

The next problem was how to crawl down without falling, perhaps injuring herself and certainly calling attention to her presence in the attic.

Then, without warning, there was a splintering crash and Veronica felt herself toppling into space. Her head struck something below, then bounced against the heavy newspaper-covered urn she clutched against her. She felt nothing more.

Somewhere in that nether world of blackness Veronica heard the muted chime of bells. Closer to her she sensed the warm bulk of what felt like a wadded electric blanket. Only, she thought foolishly, blankets didn't have tongues that licked hands or voices that whimpered with concern. She tried to open her eyes but was unable to get past the hot, pink halo of light behind her lids. With all her strength she tried to rise on one elbow, the other seeming to be pinned beneath a heavy package. The muzzle of the warm bulk pushed her back down gently but with authority.

Her eyes flew open then. "Brutus! Oh, Brutus, how did you find me?"

At the sound of her voice, the great animal sprang

to his feet and with a speed that surprised her rushed
to the partially-open door. There he paused as if to
tell her he was going for help. Then she heard the
soft padding of his shaggy paws as he hurried down
the narrow stairway leading into the hall below.

I must get up, her thoughts ran wildly. *Brutus will
find someone. . . oh, what if it's his master? He has warned
me to stay out of his affairs.* And that he was involved
was no longer a question. She only wondered how
deeply . . . .

Again, Veronica tried to rise on an elbow but, with a
little moan, sank backward when a zigzag of pain shot
through her temple. The blackness from which she had
recently emerged was beckoning. For a moment Veronica
fought against it, then, deciding that it was to be preferred
to the stabbing pain in her head, she let its long dark arms
envelop her.

It was all an incredible dream, of course. Soon it would
go away. And with it would go this person leaning over
her speaking little words of endearment. The deep voice
would fade. . . the warm arms that lifted her head would
melt away. . . and the face that went with it would vanish.
And she would forget it all.

Well, almost all. Not the kiss. Its memory she would
cling to, bringing it with her when she emerged from
the dream. Because she had never been kissed like that
before.

"Stay. . . *stay*. . ." she begged of the memory.

But it was the deep, rich voice that answered. "I will
always stay with you, my dear Mrs. Devonshire—always.
Until death do us part, isn't that what we pledged? But
only since you invited me—"

Veronica opened her eyes with an effort, trying to
focus them in a glazed, half-lidded stare. In the dim
light of the bare bulb, the face above hers was in half-
shadow. But there could be no mistaking the craggy

jaw, the thick brown hair glinting red in the light, and the penetrating eyes—sometimes stony but now alive with amber glints of concern. And tenderness. Tenderness? It *had* to be a dream. Through wooden lips, she tried to speak.

"Who—what?"

His answer was an amazingly gentle kiss. But it still had to be a dream. It was impossible that she would be kissing him back!

Recovering her wits, she struggled against the strength of Holman Devonshire's chest and tried to push herself free. "Let go of me this minute!"

For answer, her husband scooped her effortlessly up in his arms as if she had been a rag doll. Then, without another word, he eased his way down the stairs. There was no recourse but to relax against him, feeling helpless, ashamed, and foolish. And, for some unknown reason, still clutching the one item she had removed from the crate in the attic.

The two of them reached her bedroom. In her foggy state of mind Veronica found herself wanting the man to go and yet willing him to stay. Surely she had a concussion. Maybe permanent brain damage!

But Holman Devonshire pulled a light blanket over her and left the room. Confused, she tried to doze. It was no use and it was with relief that she greeted Dr. Gillian a short while later. "Sound as a dollar," he decided, "but pig-headed—like Hugh!"

When she awoke the next morning Holman, according to Hilda, was gone again. She hardly knew if she should be glad or sorry. There was so much that needed to be discussed. But her cheeks burned with the memory of his kisses and her own vulnerability. Resolutely she decided to put the silly episode out of her mind. Her playboy-husband was toying with her affections just as he did with the brittle women in his glittering world. So thinking,

she hardened her heart against him again and, in spite of
Dr. Gillian's orders and her still-aching head, went on with
her touring schedule.

A busy week went by. Between tours, she managed a
longer-than-usual visit with her mother. Maybe if they
could talk . . . it was no use, of course. Mother was in surprisingly good humor, true, but it was for the wrong
reasons. A fashion book lay across her lap, her room was
redecorated entirely to her liking, and there was talk, she
said, of another elegant party soon. Veronica was forced
to admit to herself that Holman Devonshire was right.
Eleanore Rosemead was a remarkably beautiful woman,
but she was fickle, something her father either overlooked or forgave. Fickle enough to fall under the spell
of the intruder who had taken from them their last shred
of self-respect in order that he, himself, could maintain
a respectable household for whatever front it was that
covered his true purpose in being in the small East-coast
village.

One would think the woman would have a shred of
pride. But there Veronica's tired mind gave up trying to
figure out the two of them—Mother and Gilbert. One
would think her brother would hate the sight of Castle
Loma's new owner. Undoubtedly, he did. But not enough
to do anything about it—

Veronica brought herself erect as she talked with her
Mother in the always sunny, now elegantly so, *chambre.*
(Mother now used as many French words as her vocab-
ulary afforded.) *I have no right to be thinking of my family
in unfavorable terms,* Veronica reminded herself, *or to be
suspicious of them.* Nevertheless, she needed to know what
had become of her brother. Something could have happened again which needed their help. And with her husband's disdain of him—

"Mother," Veronica twisted her handkerchief as she
sought the right words to ask of her mother's favorite,

"have you any idea where Gil is—I mean, he has been gone longer than usual—"

Eleanore laid the fashion book aside with a sigh. "Veronica," she said crossly, "I do wish you would stop fidgeting. And, as for your brother, I would think you would leave the boy alone. There is no need for him to be gainfully employed."

Veronica hesitated before answering. It hurt that her mother was less concerned with Gilbert's whereabouts—maybe his safety, considering his waywardness— than with the false paradise in which they were living. Her mother was lapping the luxury up as a fat cat would lap up a bowl of rich cream. She personally resented, even while admiring, the changes at Castle Loma. But her brother was another matter. He had no right to take advantage—

At that thought Veronica felt color rush to her face and she turned away lest the prying eyes of her mother detect something. Why on earth was she defending Holman Devonshire anyway? It was his idea . . . on the other hand, they were becoming more deeply indebted to him daily . . . living on the money he had stolen in one form or another from helpless widows and orphans if her father had been right . . . *and,* she thought quickly, *Father WAS right!*

"Mother," Veronica tried again, "I am worried about Gil—truly worried. He's no longer a boy—twenty-three is young manhood. And he's easily led—" She sucked her breath in and dared to go on. "Some strange things have been going on—valuable items missing—"

Eleanore Rosemead's classic features clouded with anger. "How dare you! How *dare* you accuse my son of—"

"Oh, no!" Veronica cried out in distress. "I didn't mean Gil! I meant that I want him protected in case there is suspicion cast on him."

Her mother's tapered fingers massaged her forehead delicately. "Ring for Hilda, Veronica," she said wearily. "You have exhausted my patience. I am in need of a cup of tea."

"Yes, Mother," she answered sadly.

There was no need to bother her mother again. About Gilbert. About *anything*. Her every wish had come true. Never mind the price. Or who paid. Wearily, she walked down the stairs in search of the house-keeper.

• • •

In the days that followed there was no sign of Thurman either. He was around, Hilda said vaguely when Veronica inquired, but she did not know where he was exactly or what he was doing. It seemed strange that he only came to dinner when Holman Devonshire was there. But she gave voice to none of her concerns or specu-lations. She and her husband were to go their separate ways. That undoubtedly included the persons he had in his employ. It did not, however, include his dog. Brutus was her constant companion—tagging at her heels each time he caught her out-of-doors and often scratching at her bedroom door in the middle of the night. Of late, she had been allowing the big dog to come in and curl himself on a small scatter rug beside her bed. His presence was a comfort in the silence of the great house that seemed to be waiting for some-thing to happen—something none of humanity knew about.

On Thursday, Veronica decided to go into the village. There were a few items she needed, mostly souvenirs for the gift shop, and she wished to check with Rhoda, too. She was more likely than anyone else to know where

Gilbert might be. Then there were some posters she wished put up announcing resumption of the Sunday services.

After posting her announcement in Krista's Lingerie Shoppe and the Town Hall, Veronica summoned all the courage she could muster and crossed the narrow street wishing for the first time that the town council saw fit to modernize the village somewhat. They insisted upon leaving the place much as it was for generations before. "Changelessness in a Changing World," the travel posters boasted to encourage tourist trade more than to retain a status quo of neighborliness. The illusion filled the coffers of the city treasury, but it attracted a great number of undesirables as well as the affluent it was designed for. The casino, allowed to operate because of its great source of revenue, was always overflowing, according to all reports. And the Sea Oats, questionable in its practices for as long as Veronica could recall, continued to flourish.

This morning Veronica would have welcomed wider streets. The criss-crossing of the shadows gave a twilight look to the entire village. Chimes on the old church at the edge of the village announced 11:30. She wondered what hours Rhoda Tucker kept. Maybe the winsome cocktail waitress would not be up or the place would not be opened until later in the day. But even as she hesitated in shadows of the saloon porch, there was a rustling sound followed by the cautious opening of the door.

"Come in quick, ma'am—Mrs. Devonshire!" The breathless voice belonged to Rhoda who stood in the dank semi-darkness beckoning nervously.

The girl seemed afraid even though the large dining section of the tavern was deserted. Quickly, she moved through the maze of tables covered by overturned chairs. Daylight filtered through the cracks in the heavy drapes to reveal the shabbiness of the place. By night, when the outside shone in a blaze of gaudy lights and the inside was lighted by subtly-shaded lamps, the Sea Oats would invite intimacy. And more, Veronica felt. In her mind there was a growing conviction that the place was a front for illegal activities and corruption in general. Something involving her brother or husband.

Trying to keep up with Rhoda was difficult. Veronica bumped awkwardly into the pile-up furniture at first, but gradually her eyes became accustomed to the darkness. By the time the two of them reached a small side room Rhoda pointed out, she could see the lettering on the door. "SUPPLIES," it read. The girl put a cautious finger to her lips and pointed to an office marked "PRIVATE."

Still wondering why they were here, Veronica suddenly realized her position. This was not a place "decent women" frequented . . . the streets would be crowded when they emerged and people would spot her and talk, something she must avoid in order to keep her commitment to her husband. The closed door might open at any given moment, exposing them to goodness knows what . . . and, why was she gullible enough to be led here anyway?

She was about to whisper a question to Rhoda. But the cautious finger remained at her lips and there was a haunted look in the great, colorless eyes. She had been crying. Veronica could see the telltale signs in the puffiness of her face and the red lids of the frightened eyes. And on her arms there were mahogany-colored bruises! Who had done this terrible thing—and why?

But there was no more time for questioning. Rhoda had swung the ill-fitting door open to the supply room. At the small creak of protest from the hinges, both girls jumped.

Rhoda checked the halls, seemed satisfied, then motioned for Veronica to follow.

There was a bad moment when Rhoda turned a low-volt flashlight into the darkest corner. For there, beneath what looked like grain sacks, lay the unmistakable body of a man.

The figure was so still and looked so limp that Veronica wondered if the man were dead. Well, no matter who it was, he was in need of help. Not taking time to wonder if she should become further involved, she bent down to examine the partially-covered face.

"Gilbert!" The startled cry was torn from her throat.

Rhoda hovered anxiously above Veronica and Gilbert for a moment, then tiptoed to the door to check the halls again. When she seemed satisfied they were not being watched, the girl returned.

"I've been waitin, ma'am. And I had no way to get word to you. He's been bad, Mrs. Devonshire—real bad—talkin' out of his head about things he ought'n be revealing. The count was here but refused to allow a doctor—"

Her husband knew and didn't tell her. Even refused help for a perhaps dying man. Was there no end to the cruelty within him?

Aloud, she said, "What happened, Rhoda?" Then, remembering to lower her voice, "Is this a gunshot wound—and how—"

Rhoda squatted beside her as Veronica felt for and found a pulse.

"He come here ahead of me the night of the grand party. The count, he come after Mr. Gilbert, but it was no use. He has a wild temper sometimes—" The girl paused to hold out her bruised arms.

"*Who*, Rhoda? My husband surely did not—"

"Oh, no ma'am!" Rhoda protested quickly. "And

he never meant me harm. It was just the alcohol—
and his losses—and the men—"

Veronica wanted to find out more, but time was of the
essence. Somehow the two of them must get her brother
out of this place and out of danger.

Rhoda seemed to have read her thoughts. "It's no use,"
she said shaking her head hopelessly. "He ain't going to
make it. I know the signs—the wound's turned bluish. And
we couldn't drag him out—"

Rhoda stopped in mid-sentence and Veronica felt her
own heart begin to pound against her ribs. Upstairs there
was the muffled sound of footsteps.

"Is there a back way out, Rhoda—a fire escape—
anything?" she whispered.

"No—well, just a crawl hole that nobody's supposed to
know about. It leads to the cellar and now and then the
boss lets somebody deliver—"

The girl clapped a quick hand over her mouth, but
Veronica said reassuringly, "It's all right, Rhoda. Nobody's
going to know what you have told me. Just help me while
there's time!"

Somehow they did manage with Veronica tugging at
her brother's shoulders while trying to support his head
and Rhoda trying to hold up the dangling feet. If there
were any noise . . . but Veronica refused to think about
that. Pausing every step to catch her breath, she worked
feverishly, until at last they reached a trap door toward
which the other girl pointed. Somehow they pulled him
through it.

Outside, the sun was shining brightly—too brightly.
Veronica now wished with all her heart that they were
in the protection of the shadows on the other side of
the building. There was no way she could get Gilbert
to the automobile parked two blocks away. Even if she
could drag him, they would be detected. He would be
hurt by some assailant, whoever it was, and she would

have behaved unseemly in the eyes of her husband. She shuddered, wondering which of them faced the worse fate.

Rhoda, afraid she would be missed, was trying to crawl back through the hinged door. Veronica felt a deep pity for the girl and a deep appreciation as well. She must not add to the girl's problems. But there was something she must know.

"Rhoda," she whispered, "tell me who did this and why."

The girl cowered. "I don't know, ma'am. I really don't—a stranger to me. It was over a gamblin' debt and the watchman was there—you know, the one at the grand party—both of them was goin' out on the boat," her frightened eyes searched the streets, "and they'd kill me if they knew."

It was all a deep mystery. Who were "they"? Where did Gilbert get money to gamble? And what did the boat have to do with it? And the watchman. But one look at her brother's pale face and the dried blood that appeared to be dangerously near his heart were of much more importance. So was Rhoda's safe return.

Veronica reached out a hand to touch Rhoda who was already halfway through the crawl hole. "Thank you, Rhoda," she whispered softly. "No matter how all this turns out, you have done a fine thing—a real act of Samaritanism."

But Rhoda only looked at her in bewilderment.

"Never mind, Rhoda. I'll tell you about the Good Samaritan one day. Just know that it was a Christian act you did."

The girl's plump face lighted up as she said in awe, "Have I now, Mrs. Devonshire? Me—I'm not nothin'—but have I really?"

And with that, she was gone. Veronica felt an upsweep

of joy even though the circumstances around her were all but impossible.

Oh, Lord, she prayed silently, *nothing is impossible with You. Help me now—oh, dear God, WHAT am I going to do?*

She tried to pull her brother's limp body forward, but it was no use. It had been almost impossible for the two of them to move him. Alone, there was no way. And besides she was exhausted and her head ached from the recent fall. Hopelessly, she leaned over Gilbert's chest, and began to cry.

It was then that a firm hand gripped her arm. Her heart seemed to miss a beat and then stop. They had been detected. Oh, what was she to do now?

"You never cease to amaze me, you little idiot!"

Veronica's breath caught in her throat. She had expected to hear an unfamiliar voice. Maybe an officer's. Or maybe a masked man ready to put a gun to her brother's temple and then her own. But not the voice of Holman Devonshire. Not knowing whether to be relieved or more frightened, she could only stare up at him as if they had never met before. He would poke fun at her. Say her brother deserved to die. Send her away—a sob caught in her throat, threatening to take her breath away.

But the sob never materialized. To her surprise, her husband's voice was gentle with concern. "Are you all right, Veronica? Are you able to drive?"

"Home? I can't leave my brother." The words were no more than a whisper.

"I didn't mean that. I meant able to drive my car the half-block from where it's parked around the corner. We have to move Gilbert from here in a hurry. We could be detected any time—can you drive?"

Veronica nodded, not trusting her voice.

He fished in his pocket for the keys and handed

them to her. "Keep behind that building," he said in a low voice, nodding to a vacant structure directly in front of where the three of them were. "You will be safe, but you must hurry. I'll drag Gilbert between the two buildings—what are you waiting for?"

Veronica ran the short distance although her legs felt as if they would crumple with every step and her breath came in short gasps. Fumbling, she unlocked the door of the late-model sedan. Its quiet motor started immediately and she was back with the two men in no time at all. With seemingly no effort Holman hauled her brother into the back seat.

"Scoot over quickly and let's go!"

"My car—"

"I'll take care of that later. You're in no condition to drive home."

He was used to giving orders. And having them obeyed. Probably used to dragging lifeless bodies around, too. Veronica was too exhausted to do anything but obey. He was probably responsible for Gilbert's injuries, but at least he was helping her get him home. Shouldn't they check on him?

Turning around as her husband eased the big car down the alley, Veronica was about to check her brother's pulse when something caught her eye. A movement. And she wasn't exactly sure where. There was just a sensation that something had moved. Then she saw the outline of another man, his body flattened against the vacant building by which Holman's car had been parked. Even in the shadow, the tall, thin frame looked familiar. Then a sudden shaft of light reflected from the rearview mirror reflected the silver hair.

Thurman!

Stifling the little gasp, Veronica forced herself to turn around and settle back against the velour upholstery. Her friend's presence—no, her husband's attorney, both or neither?—added another tedious subplot to the already complicated mystery. So much was unsolved that she had no idea where to start when the time came. And right now she should be asking questions of the man beside her. But she was too weary. All she wanted to do was relax against the comfort of the sun-warmed seats, lean her head back, and, forgetting all the dangers surrounding her, put her trust in a man she distrusted. The noonday sun slanted in to brush her arm then careess her cheek as the car eased around the curves up Enchanted Hill.

She must have dozed, for in no time at all there was a light hand on her arm. "We're home, Veronica."

Home? Home meant love, warmth, security. Home meant peace....

Disjointed thoughts fought their way to the surface of her sleep-drugged brain. Then in fantasy, she saw a white cottage with geranium-filled windowboxes, a fat, brick chimney sending up tendrils of smoke. There would be the smell of gingerbread baking...the sound of laughing children with sunbeams dancing in their hair....

The fantasy ended abruptly when she looked up to see the Castle Loma, its gray, time-worn battlements and towers reaching toward the stratosphere. For one foolish second it was if she had never seen the great, rambling building before. Strangers occupied it.

"I would feel lost, living there," she said thickly.

"You are, my darling," Holman Devonshire said sadly. "You are."

Chapter 8

When Veronica awoke again, she was in her own bedroom with no clear memory at first how she came to be there. Thinking it was morning, she felt for her robe quickly. She must hurry. The tours should be in progress. Not finding her robe, she rose on an elbow to check her watch and found herself fully clothed. But before her eyes could focus on the position of her hands, there was a single stroke from the ship's bells. It was past noon and certainly it was not evening yet. It must be four o'clock in the afternoon!

Jumping to her feet, Veronica ran a quick hand over her rumpled clothing. Then, as she tried to secure her wayward hair with heavier pins to avoid the time combing it took, she attempted to piece together the earlier events of the day. The visit to the Sea Oats...Rhoda's help...Gilbert's injury. *Gilbert!* She must check on her brother!

She was about to open the door and hurry to Gilbert's

room when she noticed an envelope propped on the small, marble-topped table at the entrance. Puzzled, she opened the envelope, slashing her finger with the sharp edge of the flap in her hurry. Biting on the injured finger to ease the pain, she read the note quickly:

> Veronica:
> Please let me know as soon as you are awake. It is imperative that we talk before you see anyone else—and that includes your brother. Most especially, your brother.
>   Ever your loving husband,
>   Holman

Her loving husband, indeed! Even in a sealed note the bullying man played his part well for the sake of possible prying eyes or to mock her. She wondered anew how much longer she could carry out her end of the bargain, put up with his largesse toward her and her family, and ignore what could only be interpreted as his criminal acts.

With a determined hand on the knob, she opened the door a crack then closed it. She couldn't see Gilbert until she had seen her husband. The note was an order. One she dared not disobey.

Well, how was she supposed to notify him that she was "available"? Ringing for Hilda would be the best way. Veronica put the idea away. It seemed wiser to involve as few others as possible to this strange husband-wife relationship. The only solution was—*perish the thought!*—to go to his room.

A few minutes later, she rapped softly at his door, half-hoping there would be no response. But the door opened almost immediately, as she should have known it would. Holman Devonshire knew she would meet his demands. She was his collateral in every sense.

For a moment, however, Veronica imagined a flicker of surprise in his gold-flecked eyes. Then he opened the door wider and whispered cordially, "Come in, my dear—the first time you have visited my quarters, I believe?"

"You know very well that it is!" Veronica said, entering with as much dignity as the situation would allow.

"My pleasure. I should have some brandy to offer."

"I don't drink. You know that."

Holman Devonshire smiled, then sobered immediately. "Neither do I as a matter of fact. And you *didn't* know that."

There were times when she didn't know this man at all. Maybe she never would know all about him. But she knew enough from what her father had told her. And the rest was easy to guess.

"I—I need to know about Gilbert," Veronica said uncertainly, aware that she was standing awkwardly in the center of the room.

"Gilbert is fine. Men like him don't die easily! Now, now, don't arch your back at my words. I didn't, contrary to what you may believe, leave his welfare to happenstance. He was then and is now receiving treatment—oh, not the kind he deserves, to be sure—"

"Treatment? You mean Dr. Gillian is with him?"

"Has been. The good doctor is now looking after your mother's needs."

Ignoring what sounded like jibes at her brother and mother, Veronica cut in quickly. "How *is* my mother? This must have been a terrible shock. What is Dr. Gillian doing for her?"

Holman smiled. "Playing cribbage with her. And now let's talk about us."

"Not about *us*. About you." Her words came out stiffly.

"Interesting topic," her husband began with his usual banter, then seeming to sober from something about her face, he changed his tone of voice in his usual chameleon-like manner. "You are wondering about your brother's wounds."

"And how you fit into the picture."

"That, my dear, is not your affair. Our contract protects me, remember?" At her mute nod, he continued, "But I can tell you about Gilbert's brawl. Little different from his usual escapades, only each growing a bit more violent. The usual gambling, losing, then drawing a gun to try to recover his losses."

When Veronica said nothing, Holman speculated, "You're wondering how he comes by gambling money?"

She nodded again. "Yes," she admitted, "and how he came to be at the Sea Oats. Isn't it supposed to be a bar—of sorts?"

"Rhoda dragged him there from the casino, though why the poor girl bothered is beyond me. I was at the Sea Oats on business and she told me. The doctor would be compelled to report gunshot wounds, so he treated by remote control. Antibiotics. Fortunately, the bullet had gone through the rib cage missing any vital organs. But for a while there was blood poisoning—"

At Veronica's sudden start, he said reassuringly, "No need for alarm. It's all cleared up now. Close call. Could be he'll learn from this one—although I doubt it. Incidentally, why don't we sit down?"

Veronica was about to refuse when she felt herself being pushed gently but firmly onto a large leather-upholstered couch. Something new. As were the hangings on the walls, the new shelves for his countless portfolios and books. Admittedly, the man had good taste. Then suddenly her eyes stopped their slow round of the room and focused on an enormous book which lay open on a fruitwood stand made especially for it. The gold lettered, thumb-indexed pages, and the long, purple-ribbon book marker could mean only one Book, the Bible.

Holman's eyes followed her. "You look surprised."

Nothing he did should surprise her, but the open Bible did. There was no need to answer. She knew that her face had shown open surprise.

"I did study for the priesthood, you know."

"What changed your mind?" Veronica hadn't known she would ask the question. And there was so much more they should be talking about. But the question seemed important.

Important or not, she was not to receive an answer. "It's a long story," Holman's voice was not unkind. "One I won't go into now."

"I shouldn't have asked," Veronica murmured.

"On the contrary, you should be able to ask whatever you wish—as long as your questions have nothing to do with my private affairs." He hesitated then added, "I wish we could be friends, but I suppose that is impossible?"

Veronica felt her back stiffen. "You know it is."

Holman Devonshire sighed. "Yes, it is—at present. Some day—" But there he stopped. When he spoke again, it was to change the subject. "I was very proud of you the night of the party. You conducted yourself beautifully. Under different circumstances—"

"Under different circumstances you wouldn't be here. Now, may I go in and see my brother?"

Her husband rose, offered her a hand, and nodded. "Of course, and may I suggest that you question him as little as possible. He will only become more sullen and somewhere along the way the man's going to have to shape up and cooperate."

There was a bit of a threat in his voice. She must caution Gilbert that he was on thin ice. Not that it would do any good. In many ways, Holman Devonshire was right about him—and about a good many other things at the Castle Loma, much as she hated to admit it.

At the door, she paused. "Holman—I—I want to thank you for looking after Gil. I'm sorry about the trouble he has caused."

For a single moment there seemed to be a sort of understanding between them. And then he spoiled it. Shrugging, he answered, "Don't thank me, my dear. He's a part of my property, too. I have no choice but to look after him—for the time being."

Tightening her lips, Veronica walked out the door and down the hall. *One day,* Holman Devonshire, *you will not be burdened with us. You'll make a slip—and I will be there waiting.* But for the first time the promise to herself did not bring a sense of satisfaction. Whatever could be the matter with her anyway!

Neither was she able to get any satisfaction from her brother. Now that he was on the road to recovery, Gilbert took on his whimpering, self-pitying tone. As usual, he was the wronged party and no amount of reasoning did any good. When Veronica saw that she was doing more harm than good, she decided against cautioning him as she had planned. Maybe Holman Devonshire was right. She should let him grow up.

With that thought Veronica turned to leave. At the door, she paused. Nobody had told her yet how her brother came by the gambling money.

Turning to face Gilbert, she made a last effort to communicate. "How did you manage the money, Gil? You do not work and we have no income. We are at the mercy of Holman Devonshire.''

The face above the recently-smoothed blanket was frighteningly pale, but the voice held the familiar snarl. ''Then ask *him*!''

''I did. But he gave me no answer.''

''How like the man—regular spawn of the devil!''

Gilbert's pale face took on a feverish glow. She shouldn't be upsetting him...and she should not care what he said of the man she hated. But reasoning was no good. And unreasonable anger rose within her breast, one that would not be put down.

''Watch your language, Gilbert. We are in his debt—and besides—''

When her anger began to cool, Veronica's words faltered. She was painfully aware of her brother's burning eyes on her. '' 'Me thinks the lady doth protest too much!' '' he taunted. Then, sinking back weakly, he gave a hollow laugh. ''Why, you're falling in love with the scoundrel. What would Father say?''

''Leave our father out of this—oh, Gilbert, can't you see what you've done—and continue to do?''

''You *are* in love with him!''

''He is my husband.'' Veronica felt her chin jut out.

''Sold to the highest bidder! Mother's right. Father was a poor businessman. Now, if you'll go away, I'll try and find peace—''

Her brother's voice trailed off weakly. But for the first time, although she felt concern for her younger brother—both physically and spiritually—there was no pity in her heart. Just sadness. And despair.

On the Fourth of July, by family tradition, there would be a picnic and barbecue at the Castle Loma. Veronica did not know whether to be glad or sorry. She ought to be glad to have the tradition revived. Her father's prolonged illness, her mother's infirmity, and the lack of money had forced discontinuation of the celebration. It surprised and, in a sense, pleased her that Holman wished to hold the picnic this year.

But memory of the last party was fresh in her mind. The thought of another large gathering was frightening. Maybe they should postpone it another year, she protested vaguely when Holman approached her about the guest list. When he asked why, she could give him no good reason.

"Then go over the menu with Hilda. No, better yet, let's go over it first," he had suggested during the evening meal. Thurman, she noticed, concentrated on his parfait. She had not seen the man since catching sight of him in the village—if, indeed, she had. But Mother was excited, Veronica saw. Another party!

"Let's see," her husband said when Thurman excused himself and Hilda had helped Mother into the electric lift for going upstairs to retire. "Let's consider vichyssoise, Beef Wellington—very rare—souffle, ices—are you listening?"

At her nod, he said softly, "Listening but not agreeing."

Veronica hesitated. When she spoke, it was to say truthfully, "I am remembering the old days. We used to have pots of steaming lobster, sweet corn, watermelon and coffee—lots of coffee—" She stopped quickly, a little embarrassed. How ordinary and unimaginative she must sound. And she was sure that for a moment she had worn a look of animation. How dull she was compared to other women. . . .

When her husband was silent, Veronica looked up. She would agree to his menu and escape. But something in his eyes surprised her. He wasn't laughing at all. He looked. . .what *was* the look? She had seen it before. . .a long time ago. . .and in the eyes of her father when he had done something to please her.

"You know," he said slowly, "I think that's what we'll do. No muss. No fuss. Just a plain, old-fashioned barbecue."

"Oh, could we?" Veronica's excitement returned.

"We can and we will."

The smile she gave him was genuine. "You have been generous in many ways—" Then, for some unaccountable reason, tears blurred her vision. Turning away quickly, she said, "There's one problem—"

"Name it."

"The fourth is on Sunday. I had planned to resume services and the posters are up. Should we wait until Monday?"

"No reason to wait. The guests can come, too. I've always thought it a shame that society somehow reserves Christianity for 'the poor.' "

• • •

July Fourth dawned bright, clear, and arched in blue. *Perfect.* Except for the feeling of apprehension that knotted into a tight ball in the pit of Veronica's stomach. She was unable to finish her English muffin and sloshed half her coffee down the sink. It had to be fear of the crowds. Trying to integrate Holman's glittering friends into her own small world of a few close friends and possible tourists and villagers who came out of curiosity was a challenge greater than she had faced before. But there was something bigger, a sense of premonition. Her family seemed to be speeding backward. Small figures in the past. Her husband loomed larger than life. And she was caught in the middle. . . .

Guests began arriving surprisingly early—even Holman's friends who, Veronica would have supposed, were late risers. Before the ship's bells chimed eight,

people were wandering about the gardens although
the service was not scheduled until ten o'clock. Veronica dressed quickly, choosing a natural linen suit with
a pleated skirt. Later in the day, she would change
from the lilac silk blouse into a more casual top—or
maybe linen pants, a part of the ensemble. Holman
had said she was one of the few women who should
wear pants. And it was important to him how she
looked. She dressed her hair with care, adding jeweled
combs.

The assembly room filled, then overflowed. Veronica asked James to open the doors between the great
room and library. When the library filled, she
suggested opening the galleries. If most of the guests
came out of curiosity, so be it. Maybe it would be the
first time that many of them had heard God's Word
read. Unaware that she herself was the center of attrac-
tion, she went about her job without self-conscious-
ness. Even when she saw members of her husband's
jet-set friends coming in, she was unruffled. Clumsy
and awkward as Mother had taught her to believe herself to be, she was uncomfortable at sophisticated parties. But when it came to the Lord's work, she was un-
flappable.

And Veronica was aware suddenly that her composure
showed. She saw eyes of some of those who had, she
knew, pegged her as being a character straight from the
Renaissance, make a new assessment. She faltered only
one time and then she recovered quickly. In the front hall
stood the fruitwood stand, centered by the Bible she had
seen in her husband's room yesterday. Casually, she
allowed her eyes to survey the faces before her, but his
was not among them.

Neither was her mother's. She chose to rest longer in
order to "appear bright-eyed" later, Hilda explained. Gil,
of course, was unable to come down. Not that he would

have. But Thurman Shield was in the crowd and Veronica saw that he was elbowing his way to where she stood, about to open with prayer.

She waited. "Do you need someone to play the organ?" he asked.

"Why, that would be wonderful!" she answered, keeping her voice below the pitch of the voices around her.

Without the aid of a hymnal, Thurman's nimble fingers moved along the keyboard, filling the halls of the Castle Loma with unexpected music. There was silence and Veronica could see amused glances changing first to interest—*here is something new!*—and then to awe. Silence fell over the audience.

When the singing commenced, one voice—a throbbing soprano—rose a good two octaves above all the others. Somehow Veronica knew even before she spotted the girl in the back row of the hall that it would be Rhoda Tucker. She knew, too, that other eyes were following her own. There would be talk. And some cold shoulders. But Veronica's would not be among them.

Veronica chose Psalm 66 for the Scripture reading. "Make a joyful noise unto God, all lands," she read and then paused. A few in the audience who had attended before recognized the signal for them to read the second verse.

As the responsive reading continued, the crowd began to add their voices one by one, making use of the hymnals she had placed in the chairs for the purpose. The volumn of their voice swelled and her heart swelled with it. Surely this was the joyful noise the Lord had in mind. And it came in some cases, she felt, from people who had never read a passage from the Bible before.

Afterward, she turned to the Book of Luke and read

the account of the Good Samaritan. In completion, she read Chapter 10, Verse 36: "Which of these three, thinkest thou, was neighbour unto him that fell among thieves?"

"The one that bandaged the wounds, I bet!" The voice was Rhoda's.

There was a little intake of breath that the girl had taken the question literally. Then, the beginning of amused laughter which would spread quickly unless it was checked immediately.

Veronica lifted a silencing hand and answered quietly, "You are right, Rhoda. And in the words of Jesus, 'Go ye and do likewise.' "

The girl's face lighted up almost iridescently. And as the others rose and began little conversation among themselves, she rushed to where Veronica was closing the Bible and preparing to greet the guests and explain the activities of the day.

"I have to get back, Mrs. Devonshire and oh, I want to thank you! But," she lowered her voice, "there's something I have to be telling you. There's going to be a delivery—I mean," Rhoda stopped, aghast at her own words, "I—I mean there's gonna be trouble—"

Rhoda, looking like a frightened animal, turned and would have fled except for Veronica's detaining hand. "Where, Rhoda?" she whispered. *"Where?"*

"The Sea Oats—the ship—"

Suddenly, Holman Devonshire appeared from out of nowhere. His eyes were ablaze and his voice dangerously low. "Come with me, Rhoda," he ordered. "I will take you home."

Before Veronica could recover from the surprising events, Thurman Shield was at her side. "Carry on as if nothing's happened, Veronica," he cautioned. "Then, as soon as possible, I must talk with you."

Numbly, she nodded and gave him quick directions

to her Secret Garden. Nobody knew about the place. Maybe it would afford privacy.

Somehow she must manage to carry on, arousing as little suspicion as possible. But this night would change her life. Of that she had no doubt. Until then, her bargain was to be a charming hostess.

Chapter 9

Thurman reached the appointed spot before Veronica. It had taken some doing to get away. Mother had insisted on being settled on the sun porch with "a few amusing people" around. Gilbert had been restless and querulous. Why must he be imprisoned? And then he had demanded to know the names of as many of the guests as she could remember. Had any of them asked for him—especially any strangers? He seemed both disappointed and relieved when she told him there had been no questions.

At first, she thought Thurman was not there. Veronica felt no impatience. Even though the feelings of foreboding persisted, it was good to have a moment alone. The sun was slipping down out of the sky. Long shadows grew and stretched out over the aster beds to rest on the ridges of sand below the ivy-covered seawall that held the garden in tact. A little breeze whispered in the palms above her head and rustled the dried grasses at her feet. When Thurman came, maybe they could enjoy a sunset together.

But the way he leaped from the bench behind the clump of uncropped boxwood said there was no time to enjoy anything. There was a sense of urgency about his manner, something having nothing to do with sunsets, secret gardens, or the way the light turned his white hair from silver to gold. Time, his quick glance at the watch on his left arm said, was more important than any of these.

"Are they taken care of?"

The guests, she was sure by the nod of his head toward the upper gardens. Yes, they were all right. Busy with removing lobster from the shells without the aid of a waiter. . . but what was so important?

"Veronica, there is no time. Maybe less than you think. It is important that I make my position clear—reveal my identity—"

Veronica felt her head jerk up. Frightened by his almost frenzied tone, she murmured, "What is it, Thurman? What do you mean?"

"I am not who I appear to be, an attorney looking for a peaceful place to open a small practice. There are some things I will be unable to explain, but you must try to understand that I have not intended to deceive you. It is not by accident that I came to be your hus—Holman Devonshire's attorney. I sought him out."

"What are you saying?" she whispered. "Did you two know each other?"

"Quite the contrary. But first, let me explain that I came to the village with a set of papers saying I had been disbarred—"

"*Disbarred?* And you are practicing *here*?" Her mouth was so dry it was hard to get the words to come out clearly.

Thurman ran a nervous hand through his hair and glanced upward to where the din of voices said that

the party was progressing nicely without its hosts before
answering. "That's what the papers said, but they were
my cover."

*Cover? I don't understand, Thurman. Make me under-
stand,* Veronica's eyes begged, but she could find no
voice.

"I am with the Federal Bureau of Investigation, sent
here to check out the count's business affairs. You
must have known that he is not all he appears to be."

*What does he appear to be, Thurman? Tell me. I don't
know*—Veronica was too stunned and too confused to
speak. She could only stare blankly at Thurman Shield
as the sun disappeared in a flame of orange in the western
sky.

Veronica realized then that the man beside her was
speaking and that she had missed most of what he said.
"—then you can come away with me and we'll start a new
life."

"Come away with you?" she asked dully. "But I'm
married."

Thurman cast a quick look at her and there was a question in his steel-gray eyes. "There is no problem with
divorce—"

"But there is—" she began weakly. "To break one com-
mandment is to break all."

"You mean you oppose it? Surely not in this enlight-
ened age!"

Veronica turned away, hoping he would not see the pain
and bewilderment she was feeling. "But what is he
guilty of?"

"*Accused* of," he corrected. "That is part of what I'm
unable to tell you. Maybe I'll know more after tonight."

Veronica turned back to him quickly. "What about
tonight, Thurman? What is going on?"

"I can tell you nothing more—except that I must go.
People are waiting—"

"What people, Thurman?" Veronica's whisper was desperate. "I have a right to know. *Officers?*"

At use of the word, Veronica's voice changed from desperation to one of shock. "Are you—you can't be an arresting officer! You said you were not what you appeared. Does that mean you're not an attorney at all? You would *arrest* him?"

Thurman's gray eyes appraised her carefully, but she was unable to read the meaning in the usually gentle expression. He seemed suddenly a stranger. After all, what did she know of him?

"Thurman!"

At her note of insistence, he checked his watch again, seemed to consider for a moment, and then spoke carefully. "Yes, I am an officer—*agents*, we are called. But yes, I am an attorney-at-law, too. The only cover being, for security, a change of name, background, and the papers showing that I am disbarred. As to the arrest," he paused at that point, his eyes searching hers as if he were gathering evidence during a court trial. Under his gaze, Veronica flinched. Somehow she knew even before he resumed what his question would be. And she did not know how to answer.

His gray eyes narrowed as a prosecuting lawyer's might when he is about to ask the convicting question. "Would it matter?"

The question wrapped her in a blanket of depression she would not have thought possible. For the first time, she faced the possible role of widowhood—either by her husband's arrest or quite possibly his *death*. Involuntarily, she shivered.

It would be hopeless to try deceiving this shrewd man. And she nodded. "In a way I cannot explain because I do not understand."

The little breeze stopped playing in the palms. A few sleepy birds warned of nightfall. And the two of them stood in the magnolia-scented twilight without speaking. It was he who broke the silence.

"Maybe I will be able to make you better understand when this night is through. Now you should be getting back to your guests."

Oh yes, the guests. Life at Castle Loma must go on. Go on without love. Because everything was hopelessly snarled...her mother and brother were no help...her husband's life was in danger...all reputations were in jeopardy...and her few friends? Veronica wasn't sure she had any friends. Certainly not among the brittle people they were entertaining—

At that thought, she laid a quick hand on the cuff of Thurman's tweed jacket. "These people—why are they here? Are they a part of this?"

"Yes and no."

"That's no answer at all!" Veronica's frustration turned to anger. But it was wrong to direct it all at him. "I'm sorry," she added quickly. "It's just that I'm so confused—"

"I understand." Thurman's voice grew suddenly gentle. "I feel sure that there will be no pity left for Holman Devonshire after tonight. And now we must go our separate ways. I will be back to you as soon as I can, my dear, and then we will make our plans. Until then," he reached to cover her hand which, unknowingly she had dug desperately into the wool fabric of his coat, carefully unfurled the fingers, and lifted it to his lips to kiss the palm gently, "close your fingers around this kiss and tuck it near to your heart. I love you very much."

And with that, the man who called himself Thurman Shield was gone, leaving Veronica alone in the gathering darkness. Lights blinked on here and there across the gardens. The laughter above her grew more boisterous and then seemed to die away. And still she stood where he had left her. What he had said made no sense. It was just another part of the nightmare that was enlarging like a storm cloud ready to open its floodgates and destroy her world.

"I need Your promise repeated, Lord," she whispered softly. "Send me Your rainbow."

And then she shook her head sadly. It was no use. Rainbows do not come at night. Slowly she wound her way up the graveled pathway toward the dying embers of the barbecue pits. Only a few guests remained. And she was glad. No matter what they might think of her as a hostess, Veronica knew that she had to be alone. Not to give way to tears or hysteria. But to make a quick plan, because she knew what she must do.

Chapter 10

Feeling her way in the darkness, Veronica found the pull cords of her bedroom drapes. She was about to draw them before switching on a light when she saw the familiar outline of the harbor-cruising vessel, its lights sparkling against the moonless sky, moving along the bay. Something told her to wait and she was not disappointed. All too soon, the great yacht moved out to sea, its light bobbing gently up and down with the breakers until it reached a smoother surface. Then, without warning, the lights blinked once, twice, three times and disappeared as the lights went out.

Quickly, she drew the drapes and turned on the night-light, which would not be detected from outside in case anyone was watching, and changed from the split skirt to the linen knickers. There had been no time earlier in the day. She fumbled in the top drawer of her bureau for a rose-and-lilac floral print headscarf and wound it into a turban around her head. Best wear the jacket that went with the ensemble and she would need goggles.

146

At the door, she hesitated. Should she leave a note? No, she didn't dare. Neither did she dare risk checking on her mother and brother for fear of waking them and arousing suspicion. There must be no questions.

Praying that the stairs did not creak, she slipped down, opened the front door noiselessly, and stepped into the cooling night air. Starting the family car would awaken the household, so her plan was to take her ancient bicycle. It was none too dependable, but it would get her there—providing the headlight battery was not dead. It wasn't. And soon she was coasting quietly down Enchanted Hill.

The gaudy lights of the Sea Oats flashed on and off like evil eyes and, in spite of her calmness until now, Veronica felt her heart pick up its tempo. That she was courting disaster there could be no doubt. Neither was there any doubt that she was right in being here. Why? She was unable to get any further in her thinking. This was a time for acting.

Rhoda's room was in back of the bar, she remembered. If she was lucky—*very* lucky—the girl might be there. She picked up a tiny pebble and tossed it against the single small window. At its soft clink, the curtain opened cautiously.

"Who's there? And what do you want? Oh, Mrs. Devonshire, ma'am, you shouldn't be here!" The dim outline of the girl in the window seemed to shudder. Then quickly she whispered, "Come to the back door and I'll let you in."

When the door opened, Rhoda did not invite her inside. "They've been here, ma'am, but they've gone." The voice was low and frightened.

"Who, Rhoda? I must have your help"

"The count, Mr. Shield—and Mr. Gilbert himself!"

"My *brother*? He's in no condition—"

"I know ma'am." Rhoda glanced furtively over her shoulder. "Best you go—"

But at that moment there was a burst of gunfire, followed by a heavy thud, and men's voices raised in angry curses. Both girls bolted inside and dodged into the only place they knew to go. Rhoda's room. There they squatted in fear, listening to every crash and bellow and wondering what was going to happen next.

"Stop it, boys! Tonight's too important for us to waste—and I suggest we get down to business, lest my reputation be spoiled!"

There was a scrape of chairs and a chorus of coarse laughter. Veronica's eyes questioned Rhoda's in their shadowy corner. "Officer Cromwell," the waitress whispered, "only he ain't no real officer in a true sense of the word."

Then they crouched silently, listening to the revealing dialogue in the main room of the bar. "The ship's gone—probably met the sister ship by now," a male voice was saying. "And she's loaded."

"Got the pieces and the papers?" Cromwell asked one of the men standing beside him.

"Sure thing, boss. And once the connection's made—"

Lusty cheers went up almost drowning the words that another member of the group said, "—cocaine—hideout—yeah, same place—"

So that was it? The group of lawbreakers, some of them "solid citizens," had sent some kind of commodities in a ship—the cruising vessel?—out to exchange the cargo for narcotics!

Cold fear gripped Veronica's insides. She wished with all her heart she could escape. Unwittingly, she had let herself in on some terrible thing that had nothing to do with her husband, her brother, and Thurman Shield. But, even as she thought the words, her heart stopped its terrible thudding and seemed to stop beating.

Maybe they *did* have something to do with it. "Oh, dear God, no!" She was unaware that she'd spoken the words aloud until she felt Rhoda's cold hand clap over her lips in an effort to silence her.

But it was too late.

The door burst open and both girls were dragged bodily from Rhoda's airless little room into the smoke-filled bar. The rough hands holding Veronica shoved her directly toward Officer Cromwell. "Here she is boss—a right pretty thing. Come on, my little sweet face!"

Veronica was filled with fear, humiliation, and indignation. She was dimly aware that her hair had loosened from its accustomed knot and fallen in an uncontrolled cascade down her back...that her blouse was torn... and that blood oozed from scratches on her arms. Rhoda, her face white with alarm, was being shoved into the back room by the heavy hands that had brought the two women into the dark, smoky room. And men! She hadn't known there were this many of them in the village. There was only time to recognize a few and to be aware of the silver glint of handguns and rifles before the hands of the man Rhoda identified as Officer Cromwell reached out to grab her arms again, his fingernails digging deep into the already raw flesh.

"Eavesdropping, were you?" The oily-haired officer wore no uniform, but Veronica could see that his clothing was cleaner and more expensive than his hired gunmen wore.

Some distant part of her brain wished again that she had more experience with men, with the world, and with life. But another part tried to cope with the here-and-now. Pleading with these men would do no good. And she dared not show the indignation she felt. She sent up a silent prayer for help and waited with anticipation.

But the answer came so suddenly and in such an unexpected way that Veronica was unprepared. There was a hiss of intaken breath as the hands gripping her shoulders tightened. She tried to draw back, a gesture which brought her face to face with her captor. And there she saw that she had been recognized by one of the men!

"Curtsey, men! You are in the presence of royalty. The woman—pardon me, Your Highness, *lady*—is none other than the Countess de Devonshire!"

"*Contiesse*, if you please." For the life of her Veronica could never figure out how she came to make the correction in such a crisis. Especially when the title was meaningless. . . like her marriage. . . .

At her words, there was coarse laughter throughout the room as the men shuffled from the tables and bowed in mockery. Several men remained seated. "I'd rather spit on her!" one of them said.

"Oh, no, we handle this one in gentlemanly fashion," Cromwell said in a low, threatening voice. "We find out just what she knows that we don't. I've told Devonshire she couldn't be trusted. Just like her cowardly brother—"

Dimly, Veronica was aware of a door's soft opening and closing behind her. But her mind was too busy trying to absorb what she had just heard to pay attention to the sound or to Officer Cromwell's coarse words.

Holman is involved. There can be no doubt now. And Gilbert. Hopelessness and depression closed around her. The world became unreal. She was acting out an old movie she had seen. Only she, the central character, did not know how or when it would end.

But end it did. And very abruptly.

A tall, familiar figure emerged from the shadows. "Take your hands off my wife."

Holman Devonshire's word were quiet and deep-throated. But there was a definite command in them. For a moment Veronica thought the hands cutting into her bare flesh relaxed. Then Cromwell's grip tightened.

"Your sense of humor eludes me," he growled. "To release this spy would be folly."

Holman stepped closer. Veronica could feel the warmth of his breath against her hair, lifting it to fly like thistledown against her face.

"Don't be melodramatic, Cromwell. Mrs. Devonshire is not a spy."

"Keep back, I warn you!" The man's angry voice rose, but it carried no authority. Instead there was a note of uncertainty. Then, lowering his voice, he said with a sneer, "Do you mean to tell me that you trust her?"

"Implicitly."

"And you would guarantee that she would keep her mouth shut about all's she's seen and heard here to-night?"

"I'd stake my life on it."

"You may have to! Now, get this doxy out of here—"

Her husband waited no longer. There was a crack of his knuckles against the jaw of the officer. The blow caught him unprepared, as Holman obviously had hoped. Later Veronica was to say a prayer of thankfulness that the man had used the derogatory word and given her husband an opportunity to arrange a getaway for her.

"Go home," he whispered before Cromwell could regain his balance and return the blow. And he pressed his car key into her hand.

She wanted to thank him. But there was no time. She fled for the door and found his car parked in the alley. Better leave the bike. No, on second thought, better take it away. There should be no evidence left that she had been here. She hurried back to where she had hidden the old bicycle behind a clump of hibiscus.

Inside, she heard her husband's voice, low-pitched and angry, but she was unable to make out his words. There could be no doubt now that he was involved in drug trafficking and goodness knows what else.

Still, she owed him something for saving her life which he very well may have done. If only there were some way she could help him out of the situation he was facing in the barroom. *I must be out of my senses,* she thought, and turned away determinedly.

It was then that a low moan came from behind her. Veronica realized that she was just below the small window of Rhoda Tucker's room. *Rhoda!* Her heart went out in pity to the poor girl who had tried to befriend her and had been the helpless victim of a beating without any doubt. She couldn't leave without checking on her.

For the second time that night she tossed a little pebble against the window. "Rhoda," she whispered, "It's me, Veronica."

The face that appeared between the cheap curtains could not belong to the rosy-cheeked waitress! Surely, it was the face of some sub-human being. Swollen so that the features were unrecognizable, the eyes were turning purple already. Blood oozed from her mouth and Veronica thought that several of the girl's teeth were missing.

"Oh, my darling, I'm sorry!" Veronica whispered in compassion, feeling the hot, salty tears course down her own cheeks. "Come with me, Rhoda—come with me, *please.* I have a car—you need a doctor."

But the face at the window was turning slowly and pain-fully from side to side to signal *No.* "I can't ma'am. They—they'd kill me. And besides, I have to wait for 'im here."

Him could mean none other than Gilbert, Veronica realized with a sick heart. She felt a deep sense of appreciation coupled with disgust. Her brother had no right to expect anything from any of them. But all of them went on protecting him in one form or another, herself included. But not anymore!

When she spoke, her own words surprised her. Still whispering, Veronica said, "You're the Good Samaritan, Rhoda. And I promise you that there will be a reward—"

"In heaven?" The girl's voice was almost inaudible.

"In heaven," Veronica said positively, *"and* on earth. Just as soon as we can get this thing settled somehow, you and I—and the others—will work something out. You have my promise!"

"Oh, thank you, Mrs. Devonshire!" Veronica could hear a note of hope in Rhoda's pathetic gasping. "And go now—*please*—I sure don't want nothing happening to the only friend I've got. . . ."

Inside, the noise had started up again. The boisterous voices rose drunkenly, giving Veronica an opportunity to load the heavy bike into the car and start the engine, hopefully unnoticed.

She eased out of the dark alley without turning on her headlights. When she switched them on as she reached the intersection, the beams picked up the un-mistakable outline of a man, his body pressed against the wall of the vacant building as it had been on her first visit to the Sea Oats. *Thurman!* But her mind could register no surprise. Too much had happened already. . . .

Back in the sanctity of her own bedroom, Veronica
had the distinct impression that she had entered another
world. A world of normalcy. One having nothing to
do with false marriage vows, crime, cruelty, and the
mysteries surrounding it all. All that was a nightmare.

But the vision was short-lived. Someone, she saw,
had been in her bedroom. At first, she wondered how
she knew. The room was not in the usual disorder
one expects when there has been a burglar or a prowler.
To the contrary, it was *too* neat. As if someone had
tried to make sure that she would not suspect by tidying
up too well. The skirt she had tossed hurriedly across
her bed after changing was too smooth. The pillows
against the love seat were too plump and unused. Even
her bookcase was straight, each book lined up perfectly,
her Bible closed.

At first, she thought nothing was missing. Then
her eyes came to rest on the small wastepaper basket
beside her vanity. It was recently emptied of the few
tissues and the envelopes of recently-answered let-
ters she remembered dropping in it. But who? And
why? The men were all away and Hilda and James
were in and out at all times, but they would not choose
a time when she was missing in a sense to straighten
up her room. They would have been out looking for
her.

Too weary to think further, Veronica was about to
stretch across her bed and relax before showering
or dressing her wounds when something caught her
eyes. Just a small thing. But significant. Her hatbox
was moved from one end of the upper shelf of her
open closet to the other as if someone had experienced difficulty in reaching the shelf. And something
was missing from the shelf. But what could it be?

And then she remembered. That's where she had
put the heavy urn she had taken from the packing

crate in the attic. But who would want the urn? It wasn't worth the newspaper it was wrapped in. Or was it? There had been no time to examine the papers on the shipment, wherever they were. Maybe it was more valuable than she had imagined—but who cared?

Suddenly, her tired mind refused to function. All she could concentrate on was a warm shower and a soft nightie.

The warm shower relaxed her body. Then on sudden impulse, she turned the knob to "cold" and let the sting of the brisk spray beat against her flesh. It burned the spots where the man's nails had scratched her flesh, but the pain felt good—as if she needed to suffer. As Rhoda had suffered. And maybe, as her husband was suffering now. Resolutely, she put the thought aside and toweled herself dry before slipping into a thin nightgown and easing between the floral sheets. A sense of languor stole over her. She closed her eyes and would have slept except for an unmistakable sound of footsteps just outside her door. She listened without moving.

"Veronica!" Her name was only a whisper, but she recognized the voice.

She lay very still, not answering.

And then the bedroom door opened noiselessly. Too late she realized that she had not snapped the latch in place. Holman Devonshire, his tall frame silhouetted by the subdued night-light in the hall, stood in the doorway.

"May I come in?"

It was a foolish question, Veronica thought muzzily. He was already inside her room. And was closing the door quietly behind him.

"That was a foolish thing you did tonight." He switched on the small night-light and advanced toward where she lay too paralyzed to move.

"Yes, very foolish," he said when he reached the bed. "We'll talk about this, but first I want a look at those arms."

Veronica pulled the covers defensively up and held them beneath her chin. Her husband laughed in genuine amusement.

"You look like a child who's afraid to be given a measles shot!"

But Veronica did not look amused. "Keep away from me."

Holman Devonshire's hands reached out and pulled the covers from her numb fingers seeming to exert no effort. Peeling them back lower than she thought was necessary to see her shoulders, he focused his eyes on the scratches that were beginning to smart.

He frowned ever so faintly. *He looks tired, very tired,* Veronica thought. Deep circles beneath his amber-lighted eyes. Mouth tightened as if from tension. But incredibly handsome as always in the casual fawn trousers and matching cashmere sweater. No! She refused to pity him. She must protect herself . . . guard against his charm . . . harden her heart. *Too much fast living. That's what tired him out.* Why then did her heart ache?

"Stay where you are. Where's your first aid kit?"

Veronica pointed wordlessly to the chest in her bathroom.

With the practiced hands of a doctor, he swabbed the scratches, pausing only when she flinched, and then covered them with gauze. All the while, he mumbled to himself. "Clumsy oafs . . . laying hands on you . . . dirty . . . ." His voice trailed off as the job was finished.

"Are you injured anywhere else?"

"No!" She grabbed at the covers again.

"Stand up and let's make sure."

Afraid to disobey, Veronica reached for the light robe that matched her nightgown. Crawling out on the side opposite him, she pulled the loose garment tightly around her.

"I'm fine—" Then, to her complete surprise, Veronica felt the room sway. Dizzily, she swayed with it and would have fallen except for a firm hand on her shoulders as Holman sprang forward.

"Ouch," she protested weakly when her husband's hand touched one of the bandages.

"Sorry," he murmured and laid her gently back on the bed. Then, leaning over her, he looked deeply into her eyes. "Now, my dear Mrs. Devonshire, you will explain to me exactly what you were doing at the Sea Oats tonight."

Veronica had not expected the question and her voice faltered. "I—I—why, I wanted to help."

"Help whom?"

When she did not answer, he said, "Exactly how much did you overhear?"

"Nothing," she said. "I mean nothing I did not suspect already." Suddenly, the anger, hurt, humiliation, and disappointment were back to give her courage. "That you are involved in all the slime—"

"I never tried to pass myself off as a saint."

That was true. What, then, did she expect? The question led to a dead-end street she had traveled many times already. But it was imperative that she get at some answers.

"Where is my brother? Is he involved? How could you—"

Holman inhaled deeply, his nostrils flaring slightly. "I think you know the answers, Veronica, only you will not allow yourself to face the truth any more than you face the truth about your own emotions."

She tried to draw back deeper into the pillows. Then to her immense relief he looked away. "How can I get through to her?" He seemed to be addressing a third

party. "How can I make her see that her weakling brother
will never have the spine of a jellyfish unless she lets him
grow up—take it all on the chin—"

The soliloquy stopped abruptly. "You know he's
gambling heavily."

"And *you?*"

"We are talking about Gilbert at the moment. As if
gambling all this place away were not enough, the valuable
pieces are going one by one."

Gilbert? Gilbert was taking her father's collection? Only
it wasn't her father's anymore. It was—why, he was stealing from his brother-in-law! He could prosecute...drive
them all from the house....

"What are you going to do?" Her voice was but a weak
whisper.

He turned back to her. "A lot of that depends on you.
Some of your pieces are gone, too."

The *cross!* And the other pieces she had missed one by
one. The open crates. That had been her brother in the
attic. Not Holman.

The room swayed again. It was all too much. Her tongue
felt thick. But she must speak. She *must.* "Wh—what do
you mean—th—that Gil is gambling the pieces away?"

"Worse! He's gambling them away over and over—but
I can see you do not understand." When she shook her
head, he explained, "Making out false papers and forg-
ing them to sell replicas. He's been found out several times
and there will be more—some of them, the syndicate,
harder to handle. And I've fought his last battle,
Veronica."

So have I, she wanted to say. But she owed this man no
explanation.

Instead, she said stiffly, "I'm very tired. If you will go—"

"Ah, the time is not yet," her husband said, leaning even
closer. "You have not answered my question as to what
you were doing at the Sea Oats. Checking up on me?"

"I—I—would you believe me?"

"Yes, because you aren't going to lie to me, Veronica. You *were* checking on me."

Her silence condemned her, Veronica knew, but he was right. On both counts.

"Then—you know what to expect?" Holman sat down on the edge of the bed then and leaned down to brush the part of her hair with a light kiss. "It smells of peppermint, but not offensively so," he murmured as his lips moved a little farther down to touch her high rounded forehead.

The languor she had felt moments ago turned to a warm glow, signaling danger. "Go! You promised me—"

"That I would stay out of your life? Make no demands? Ah, so I did, but that was before tonight. And we both know that it was you who broke the contract, don't we?"

It was impossible to think with his fingers threading through the strands of her long hair, outlining the contours of her face, and tracing her eyebrows in their high, natural arch. "These brows make you look perpetually surprised," he whispered, "but you should not be surprised at this moment—"

"You promised never to come uninvited," Veronica whispered.

For answer, his lips claimed hers in a gentle kiss. "Your behavior tonight was an invitation." His mouth was against her ear.

"Let me go this minute!" Veronica cried out. "Let go of me or I will scream."

"That would be unwise—unless you wish to tell your mother and the servants the details of our contract. I have every right to be here as your husband. In fact, your ambitious mother encourages it. But go ahead, my dear. Scream! In which case you will have violated the terms even more—"

"Oh, stop it—*stop* it! I hate you—"

Her words were drowned out by another kiss—this one more demanding. And to her astonishment and total humiliation, Veronica found herself responding.

The moment ended abruptly. Holman Devonshire rose to his feet and pulled the covers gently over her trembling body. "Yes, I am sure you do," he said gravely. "It was not part of our bargain that you should love me, Veronica. It may come as a surprise to you that I shall keep my part of the contract—although you have broken yours. In fact, I shall make you another promise. I will not come back until you invite me—this time with words."

And with that promise, he was gone.

Veronica lay sobbing in her pillow. *I was powerless against him.* The thought frightened her more than any of the strange, horrible events that preceded it. And then she sat bolt upright in bed.

She, Veronica Rosemead, the Contiesse de Devonshire, was hopelessly in love with the wrong man. Her husband.

Chapter 11

When Veronica went down to breakfast the following morning she found Hilda alone. None of the others had come down for the meal the older woman said. Maybe this would be a good time to try talking with Mother. So thinking, she prepared a tray for the two of them while Hilda busied herself with the menu for dinner that evening.

Plucking a rose from the vase on the breakfast table, Veronica asked casually, "Have you seen Mr. Gilbert, Hilda?"

Did she imagine that Hilda's eyes were averted when she answered? "No—he didn't come home last night, Miss Veronica."

Wondering what terrible thing may have happened to him, Veronica carefully laid the rose on her mother's tray. "He was not really expected, Hilda," she said truthfully.

Upstairs, her mother sat in a sunny window of her large bedroom, her delicate features outlined against the trumpet vines that trailed along the trellis beyond. Veronica admired her from the partially-open door.

Then she knocked and entered. Eleanore Rosemead turned to greet her with a little fluttering motion, her eyes lighted with expectation. But at the sight of her daughter, the light faded. "Oh, it's you, Veronica," she said with a note of disappointment.

Veronica, trying hard to put aside the hurt her mother always brought to her heart, laid out the coffee service and made small talk. Toward the end of the meal, she said, "Mother, if ever there comes a time when we need to leave this house—"

Her mother's cup clattered to the floor. "Leave Castle Loma? Never! It is my life," she cried angrily. "Why do you insist on upsetting me?"

She was so agitated that Veronica wondered if it would be wise to help her back to bed. Her mother's next words were, therefore, comforting.

"Clear these things away. I am expecting Dr. Gillian. He is far more concerned about my well being than—most."

On the way downstairs, Veronica met the doctor and whispered that she would like a word with him before he saw her mother. They descended together to stand in the parlor which was roped off for the early-morning tour. There she explained her mother's behavior, ending with what she hoped was an explanation.

"I feel responsible. I—I—"

Dr. Gillian raised his hand as if to silence her words. Slowly, her father's friend wagged his head from side to side. "Why, oh why, my child, must you feel responsible for everything that goes on in this house?"

"I'm sorry—"

"And stop apologizing!" Then, in a softer voice, he continued, "You have so much beauty. Both outwardly and inwardly. Attributes which nobody, even yourself, seems to recognize except the two of us."

"Two?"

The doctor picked up his black bag. "Yes, two. Myself and your husband. You see, we love you."

Veronica stood frozen to the spot, her eyes glued unseeingly at the gold frames encasing the still-life paintings in front of her. Holman Devonshire loved her? That was impossible. No man who loved a woman would leave her penniless, keep her at his mercy—and then reject her!

Reject? At the thought, Veronica gasped. She had offered him nothing. So how could she be rejected?

Angrily, she hurried from the room.

By the time her first tour was finished Dr. Gillian was waiting for her in the parlor again. "How is my mother?" Veronica asked with concern.

The doctor carefully took off his glasses, wiped them, and returned them to his nose. "Better—or worse. I'm trying to decide. She was going over the old clippings, things I understood were destroyed."

Veronica waited for him to go on. It was about the night she was injured, he said. Veronica did know there was newspaper coverage of the accident? When she shook her head, he explained that the papers hadn't been too kind. That Eleanore had been most distraught over the articles. And that her husband had ordered all accounts burned.

"I don't know where the newspapers came from," he continued, obviously puzzled. "They were well preserved but rumpled as if they had been packed away—"

Packed away. The crates! Mother had been in her room...taken the vase...the newspapers. But there was no way without help. And there had been none. It was impossible...and suddenly nothing made sense.

"Are you all right?" Dr. Gillian's voice sounded far away, but she reassured him and hurried him away.

Somehow, when Mother was out for her afternoon sun, she must get into the bedroom. If the papers were there, she must read them.

The opportunity came earlier than she expected. Evalina Mancini, a frequent guest in the house since the arrival of Holman Devonshire, called to share her expertise on silver with her mother. When the two of them were seated comfortably with tea in the conservatory, Veronica murmured an excuse and hurried upstairs.

Hilda had closed the shutters against the sun in preparation for Mrs. Rosemead's nap, making it difficult for Veronica to see. But, once her eyes adjusted to the dim light, she found the newspapers stuffed in a trash can ready for emptying. She wasted some time trying to unfold them, only to find that large sections had been cut out. But of course! Dr. Gillian had said that Mother was examining the clippings. In her frenzied haste, Veronica knocked over something large and cold. The urn she'd found in the attic—so she had to be right. But what was this that spilled over the floor? On her hands and knees, she felt for the fallen objects. Then, to make sure that she had missed none of them, she turned on her mother's night-light beside her bed.

Jewels! *Valuable* jewels! Opals, rubies, a triple-strand of opalescent pearls...and the beautiful dinner ring had to be sapphire...surrounded by diamonds. What did it all mean? But its meaning was less important than the newspaper accounts at this point. So, easing the jewelry back into the urn, she replaced it on the small antique table where it had stood and resumed her search.

Time was flying. Veronica was all but ready to give up when she saw what appeared to be the torn edge of a newspaper showing from beneath one of her mother's bed pillows. She lifted the pillow and what she saw astonished her. There, staring back at her, was a reflection of herself. So real that she might have been standing before a mirror. And the picture— why, the picture was beautiful. Why would the sudden realization that she possessed her mother's beauty be important at a moment like this? Veronica did not know. Unless it meant that Mother hated her because she hated herself.

And then, knowing that her presence could be detected at any moment, she scanned the clippings. At first, she had to read and re-read to comprehend. Then the story began to make more sense, unbelievable though it was. "Eleanore Blazedale Rosemead, socialite, found at bottom of stairs...Mystery surrounding details, some of which may never be known...missing jewels. Rumors persist that the Rosemeads' marital problems, mostly relating to antics of playboy-son, may be involved. Insurance company investigating...."

Picture after picture paraded before Veronica's eyes. Her mother on yachts with other men. Baby pictures of herself and Gilbert. And then the glaring headlines: INVESTIGATION LEADS INSURANCE COMPANY TO BELIEVE THAT WIFE OF HUGH ROSEMEAD HURLED HERSELF DOWN THE STAIRS OF THE MANSION! PROBABLY ATTEMPT OF SUICIDE....

As if reading about a stranger, Veronica read on, losing track of time. And then she folded the clippings and placed them carefully back in their hiding place. The story was heartbreaking, sad, and frightening. But it was past—a place where her mother chose to live instead of visiting now and then. It was too late now.

Some of the reports were based on speculation, true. But Veronica suspected that they cut close to the bone of truth. The prominent family had been in the public eye, so Eleanore's private life may have been more innocent than implied. But Veronica had seen enough in later years to accept as fact her brother's gambling, his lifestyle, her mother's overprotection...yes, even to the point of pawning her jewels...maybe claiming them stolen. If the insurance company's investigation had been initiated by her father, it was easy to guess the rest. Her mother, given as she was to hysteria when life presented her with problems, may have tried—unconsciously perhaps—to frighten her husband, only to have the foolish act bomerang. And make her helpless. *IF it did—*

But Veronica put the thought behind her. Life must go on. There were too many other things that needed resolving. She would continue to protect her mother's image as her father had done. It would be easier now, because Mother could no longer hurt her. She felt a deep pity for the empty-hearted woman who had never known the real meaning of love.

• • •

Holman, cool and remote as if last night's episode had never occurred, devoted his attention to Mother during dinner. Surely he would make an effort to report on Gilbert. Instead, he excused himself before dessert and moments later she heard him start his car. On his way to another rendezvous at the Sea Oats undoubtedly. *Father was right,* Veronica thought bitterly, *men like Holman Devonshire never change!*

Thurman's eyes were on her. Giving him a sidelong glance, Veronica smiled wishing that she could return his love. He was so right for her. Life simply was not fair. Her thinking was cut short by a little jerk she saw of his head, an unmistakable signal for her to join him.

"If you ladies will excuse me?" He rose and turned toward the hall.

"Gilbert?" Veronica asked in a whisper when they were alone.

Thurman shook his head. "No idea where he is— or where Holman has gone," he said hurriedly. "There's an investigation underway which is supposed to be secret, but I want you to know. All evidence indicates that both men are involved heavily in smuggling and illegal gambling for the purpose of income tax evasion. One night the ship will be caught this side of international waters—"

"And the narcotics?" Too late, she realized that perhaps she had revealed something the F.B.I. agent did not know. "I mean, is there a possibility?"

"I had not thought of that. Anyway, that's not a part of my job. But, Veronica—" Thurman's voice caught in his throat as he leaned down to look into her eyes, "It is about us that we must talk. This whole situation is going to get nasty, leading to arrests and probable conviction. I do not want you to suffer from it any more than is essential."

"There's nothing I can do to avoid it."

He moved closer to place a pleading hand on her shoulder. "I want you to marry me, Veronica—to get out of this marriage which is no marriage at all. A divorce would be easy to arrange."

Veronica closed her eyes in desperation. "I've entered into a marriage contract. I took the vows no matter how empty they may sound."

"There's nothing sacred about those vows under

the circumstances. I've spoken with Reverend Crussell. Even he is willing to go along with an annulment as long as the marriage has not been consummated."

When she did not answer, Thurman lifted her hand to kiss her palm again. Then he closed her slender fingers over the warm spot where his lips had been. "You will come to love me in time. Believe me, your husband is not worth your loyalty."

"It's not just that—give me time—I am unable to think—"

A peal of the front doorbell broke into the conversation. Hilda was upstairs settling Mother for the night, so Veronica answered the ring. Thurman, with quick strides, hurried toward the back stairway.

Two strangers stood at the door. Men in plain clothes who flashed badges of identificiation. "Captain Dunkerk, Internal Revenue Officer. You are Mrs. Devonshire, I believe?" the taller one said.

She nodded as if in a dream. Then they would like to know the whereabouts of her husband. Veronica didn't know. Had he spoken of going out of the village? No, she expected him back.

The shorter man with thinning hair stepped forward to speak. "Where was your husband on the night of July Fourth?" he asked, his sharp eyes piercing hers.

Inside, Veronica bristled. Outwardly, she forced herself to be calm and composed. "Why, he was here, captain," she said innocently. "We had large party— a barbecue."

"Don't attempt to shield the man, I warn you. We took a good many of the men into our custody, but unfortunately there were no grounds for arresting your husband—at this point. All evidence points his direction."

"Circumstantial?" Veronica was surprised at herself for playing this dangerous game.

The man waved an impatient hand. "Oh, come, come! Let us stick with the point." He bent close to her face, so close that she smelled the smoky odor of a recent cigar. Then, with a near-brutal tone of voice, he fired the question. "How long was he with you last night?"

Veronica took her time replying. Deliberately, she opened the door behind the men as if she expected they would be leaving soon. Then, glancing at them coyly, she said, "That is a little personal, gentlemen. But I am willing to answer. Where, may I ask, would a recently-married man who wants to start a family be but with his wife all night?"

Her back was to the stairs, but realizing that someone was behind her, Veronica turned. Thurman stood looking at her, his face white with shock and disbelief, his eyes filled with pain.

Paying no attention to Thurman, the taller man said, "We have no choice but to accept her evidence—for now."

Obviously, they did not believe her. But she had given her husband a stay of execution. Once they were outside the door, Veronica fled past where Thurman still stood without daring raise her eyes. The full impact came to her now just what she had done. She had not told a mistruth, but she had implied that Holman had been with her all night. There could be no annulment. And her father's teaching said no to divorce.

And what had come over her anyway? The chance she had waited for to trap Holman Devonshire, her father's enemy, had come and gone.

● ● ●

In the days that followed Veronica went about her routine as if in a dream. Nothing was real except for a pair of strange mismatched eyes that haunted her. Eyes that could be cold and hard. Or tender with compassion. But always filled with life and fire. Where was their owner?

In her lethargic state, Veronica could hardly bring herself to wonder the same about Thurman, who as usual timed his absence with her husband's. Neither could she allow herself to become ill over Gilbert's disappearance. Surely, if he were a victim of foul play she would know. The men were important. But less so than her husband.

And then on Sunday Rhoda slipped into the morning worship service after it had begun. Veronica's first impression, after her initial shock, was to discover that the waitress's face was almost healed. The poor girl had undoubtedly become conditioned to such mistreatment. Then, when Veronica would have made her way to where Rhoda was seated at the back of the assembly room, she was gone. In the chair she had occupied was the Bible she had used. An envelope was tucked so that no eye could have missed it.

It took Veronica several minutes to make out the scribble and figure out the misspelled words. But the message was clear. Comforting. And frightening! Rhoda had "him" hidden. But she feared for "his" safety and her own. Officer Cromwell had been picked up, as had "the others," but they were out on bail . . . and what should she do? "But, please, ma'am, don't be risking yourself and me by coming here." The pitiful note was signed with an "R."

It was good to know that Gilbert was being looked after . . . or was it? He was a fugitive. Rhoda mustn't bear this alone. *But what can I do?* Over and over she asked herself. And she spent many hours on her

knees praying for them all and that God would give
her the strength to carry on and the widsom to know
what to do.

Thurman appeared suddenly toward the end of the
month as Veronica prayed alone in her Secret Garden.
He had heard enough to make his words a statement,
not a question.

"I can never make you happy, Veronica," he said
sadly. "I thank you for your prayers. They show that
a part of you cares—for my safety and my soul. But
how can you pray for—" He paused to sigh and then
continued softly, "Well, I have brought a partial answer
to your prayer. Your husband is alive."

Veronica sprang from her knees, but when she would
have spoken he silenced her with a palms-up gesture.
"I'm sorry. That is all I am at liberty to say."

"And Gilbert?" she whispered above the pounding of
her heart. *Holman's alive. Holman's alive. . .* it throbbed.

Thurman Shield shook his head. "Who knows? Maybe
they're together." His voice was low but bitter. "Holman
Devonshire is a cunning man. He'll always find a way
to escape a net."

And does he consider our marriage a net? Her heart's
tempo slowed.

Basically, his work was finished here, Thurman told
her. He would be going West on a new assignment.
If ever—but, no, he dared not hope that she would
change her mind. Numbly, Veronica shook her head,
only half-listening when he told her his real name
and where "home" was to him. Bodily, she stood with
him among the sun-wilted flowers. But her heart was
with another man. When at last he took her hand in
farewell, the suffering in his gray eyes tore at her
heart. *I know how it hurts, Thurman. How well I know
what it's like to be rejected by the person you love. . . .*

Sadly, she watched until Thurman Shield's car disappeared around a curve as it descended Enchanted Hill for the last time. A part of her regretted that she had been unable to help him more. There was much she could have revealed about her husband and her brother. Maybe neither deserved her loyalty or her love, but she could not endanger their lives. Maybe keeping one's word was not as all-important as her father had taught her to believe. But the other part of Veronica Rosemead Devonshire said aloud, "No, that is not true. It all begins with God and His promises. Thanks to Isaiah, His prophet, who tells us, 'The grass withereth, the flower fadeth: but the word of our God shall stand forever.' "

Chapter 12

August came in with a wall of heat that pushed against Veronica with each step she took. Charged with dangerous energy, this kind of weather made people edgy and uneasy. The mercury reached the mid-nineties and stayed there. It would take a storm to break the heat and humidity—causing the tiny explosions of air to burst into a giant one. Until now, she had managed to live with the concerns and heartaches, and the indecisions surrounding her life. The hurt had not lessened, but Veronica now knew that things were not going to right themselves without action.

She considered going into the village in spite of Rhoda's request. There was little telling what had happened to the girl and to Gilbert. And surely they would know what had happened to Holman. At that point, her heart refused to accept what her mind was feeding it. That he had been captured. Killed! Or, that having used her for whatever his purposes, he had abandoned her

173

174 · WITH ALL MY HEART

forever. And, admittedly, she had been afraid to face
that. But she must know. Try to face it. And get on
with whatever was left of her life.

She thought of sending Hilda or James with a note,
then decided against it. Not all of the smugglers and
illegal gamblers had been rounded up and the others
were out on bail. They might recognize the couple
as help from the Castle Loma. It occurred to Veronica then that she could depend on Dr. Gillian to help.
Nobody would suspect a doctor.

When he came to check on Eleanore Rosemead that
sultry afternoon, Veronica spoke with him quickly in
the hall. Her mother was fretful, she told him. The
air conditioner was not working. And Mother was
undoubtedly worried about Gilbert, a fact she would
deny. Stirring a pitcher of iced tea for him to take
up for the two of them, Veronica explained the situation quickly and asked if he would check with Rhoda
at the Sea Oats. To her immense relief, he agreed.

When the last tour was finished, Veronica paced the
floor restlessly as she waited for sight of Dr. Gillian's
ancient car. That would mean news. Otherwise...but
she dared not think of that.

Hoping to hear of a cooling trend, she tuned in on
the local weather station. And what she heard caused
a shiver to run the full length of her spine in spite
of the sweltering heat. It was unbelievable! There had
been no warning! No, that was not true. There had
been little warnings. Like those in her life. But Holman
was right. She didn't listen. Well, she was listening
now. Kneeling to hear, but keeping the radio turned
low so Mother would not become alarmed, Veronica
kept her ear tuned to the newscaster's words, her lips
forming a silent prayer.

"Of all the natural catastrophies, the danger and
potential damage are easiest to predict for hurricanes,"

the man's voice said reassuringly. "As local residents
know, the National Hurricane Center in Miami has
become skilled in tracking down these sea-born storms
and pinpointing where they will pound ashore...."

His words trailed off when there was a crackle of
static. Was there electrical activity already? Veronica looked out of the window and was surprised to
see towering banks of clouds building rapidly in the
eastern sky. Without the accustomed hum of the air
conditioning system an eerie silence hung over the
great house.

"...and people living in the vulnerable coastal areas
are advised to take precautions immediately...seek-
ing higher ground...boarding up windows...prepar-
ing for electrical outage...it's moving rapidly toward
the more rural areas along the coast...already declared a hurricane..." The radio was silent and then
the warning continued, "Hurricane Mario is expected
to strike with 115-mile-an-hour winds tomorrow somewhere in the vicinity of Laura Bay—"

Laura Bay! Where the village was situated! Veronica
could listen no more. She could only recall a similar
blow when she was a tiny child, one which took countless lives because of its ferocity and the fact that the
seawall had not held. The ocean had pounded its way
through the broken wall, a wall which had never
been replaced. Wildly, Veronica remembered that she
had never managed to get around to having *their* wall
checked for safety. It, too, might go....

Then blessedly, she heard the familiar protest of
Dr. Gillian's car as it huffed its way up the steep
slope of the driveway! She ran to welcome her friend
with an embrace that almost swept the elderly man
from his feet.

Even as she ushered him into the reception room, Veronica was aware of a premature twilight that darkened

the summer sky. The doctor loosened his tie before speaking.

"We'll talk as we prepare for the storm. It's never clear where to draw the line between frightening folks unnecessarily and not warning them early enough. You knew a storm was brewing?"

When Veronica nodded, he suggested that they have Hilda alert the rest of the household. "We'd all better leave in spite of being high on a hill. I don't trust the wall. And we'll have to hurry as the roads will be clogged."

Leave Castle Loma? She shuddered thinking of all she must do and her mother's reaction. But the doctor was right and he would need to be near at hand to care for the injured. She rang for Hilda.

"We'll go to my house at the upper end of the village," Dr. Gillian said. He had already begun to close the shutters. James would be barring the windows... and there were belongings Veronica must collect for herself and Mother. But she could not will herself to move.

"Holman—Gilbert—what did Rhoda tell you?" she said through wooden lips.

"Start moving, Veronica!" How much he sounded like Father. "We may have little time!"

As she obeyed, going from room to room, he followed, taking precautions that experience had taught him while she packed a bag. His words, as they worked, were at times drowned out by a tattoo of raindrops that seemed to explode against the window and violent gusts of wind that seemed to threaten the turrets of the castle. One such gust set the ship's bells ringing in wild symphony—their studied rhythm forgotten.

Through all the clamor and confusion, Veronica's constant prayer was one of thanksgiving that her father's friend was with her. Somehow they would manage—the two of them and God.

She crammed necessities into a hurried heap, hardly needing a light because of the constant flash of blue-white lightning zigzagging across the black sky from all directions. Its severity said the hurricane would come ashore sooner than the forecast warned.

"Rhoda's all right," Dr. Gillian's words came between howls of the wind and the heavy rolls of thunder. "So's Gilbert, thanks to her...kept him safe...but I took them away." Singlehandedly? Well, no, there was the Lord on his side. And then (with a grin she caught as a fiery-tongued flash of lightning seemed to split the world in half) the good Lord sent him an earthly helper. Who would suspect a parson? The good man surprised the owner and patrons with his appearance. Drew fire away from himself as he hustled Rhoda and Gil from the back room of the Sea Oats. Rhoda was asking Gil to give himself up....

Where were they? But the doctor did not hear. "Your husband's been hurt, Veronica, which accounts for his long absence in part—the other part being his duties and the secrecy involved."

Duties? Secrecy? How noble! But no matter what the man was, or how foolish she was, Veronica knew a secret calm and peace that no storm could destroy. Holman was safe. Oh, praise the Lord, he was safe! It was wrong to love a man like him. But love him she did.

"...investigating narcotics. Rhoda knew and was helping him..."

"Who?" Veronica asked stupidly, her mind daring not hope.

"Keep moving," the doctor growled. "Your husband, of course! He's busted the narcotics ring even though he was blasted apart in the process. Not to worry. Concussions will heal. This is the real Count de Devon-

shire," the doctor shouted, "sent here explicitly to
check out the drug traffic from Cuba—and uncovered
some other things at the same time. Investigated every-
body—even Thurman Shield."

The wind was picking up velocity. It shrieked through
the towers and outside the slender palms were bend-
ing agonizingly near the ground. James and the other
men were almost swept off their feet as they collected
everything that would move and rushed it into storage.
Nothing was real except for the warm feel of a furry
body brushing against Veronica's legs.

"Brutus!"

The great animal whined and ran toward the back
stairs. Mother! Oh, how could she have forgotten
her mother's fear of storms? The fierceness of the
storm would have awakened her. And nobody could
hear her cries above the shrieks of the wind. She
left the doctor talking and rushed to the stairway,
only to have the lights blink out all over the castle.
A replay of the night Mother had fallen. . . .

She stood for a moment, catching her breath and
trying to get her bearing. Then suddenly there was
a splintering crash somewhere above—coupled with a
hysterical scream. And there, in a fragile negligee
at the top of the stairs, was her mother. *Standing!*

It was all a dream of course, but even in a dream there
is action. When there was another splintering crash,
louder than before, it was followed by a sudden expo-
sure of eerie light from above. The roof of Mother's
room had collapsed!

"Meet me, Mother! Don't wait! There's no power
for your chair—oh, Mother—" And sobbing Veronica
ran up the stairs.

With both hands grasping the banister, slowly but
surely, her mother descended toward her. Veronica
held the trembling body close as they sobbed together

until Dr. Gillian could come to tear them apart and help Mother down the remaining stairs. A step at a time was enough. . . .

The staff had gone except for Hilda and James. The loyal pair would remain until their beloved family was safe—or perish with them. Dr. Gillian was settling Mother in his car and adjusting the air conditioning for her comfort. Hilda remained behind to help Veronica recheck locks on the undamaged part of the castle. They would not go upstairs—

Oh, but they must! It occurred to Veronica suddenly that her mother's jewels were there. "Mother's gems— I must get them—"

But Hilda's hand on her arm was firm, her voice forceful. "No!" she said with a note of authority Veronica had never heard her use. "You are not to go. It is unsafe and the jewels have caused too much heartbreak already!" So Hilda had known all along. . . .

Sick at heart, Veronica realized that the woman was right. But what would happen to Mother? *Nothing!* The answer came with new clarity. Nothing except the suffering Eleanore had inflicted upon herself. Her sins had found her out in a very literal sense and she had had to live with that Biblical truth. There had been no insurance payment, so Mother would suffer no punishment other than guilt. . . the greatest punishment of all. . . .

Forever after, Veronica was to ponder the strangeness of what followed next. But then, so many miracles had come from the storm that one more only supported her growing faith that for all things there was a season and a purpose—a Divine purpose.

As she stepped out so that James could close and bolt the double door, her ears caught the distant sound of a muffled bark. Brutus!

Freeing herself of James's restraining hand, she rushed

toward the sound. It seemed to be—yes, it was!—coming
from her room where the door had blown closed as the
great animal padded protectively behind.

Brutus almost knocked Veronica from her feet in
his joy at being freed. "Let's go, boy!" she said to
him, hurriedly reaching into the lower drawer of her
dressing table for an umbrella.

There her hand closed around an envelope in the
darkness—no, two of them. The contract, she realized.
And the envelope her husband had handed her the night
of the fateful birthday party.

Then, although the ship's bells were ringing as if in
a last warning and the lightning-lit sky might well
have heralded the end of Planet Earth, Veronica flipped
the switch of her flashlight and let her eyes scan the
paragraph underlined in red in the marriage contract
which she had signed and never read. She, the unbelievable words said, was half-owner of the Castle Loma...
and, should anything happen to her husband, all rights
reverted to her....

Quickly cramming the revealing document into her
trench coat pocket, Veronica ripped the birthday envelope open with her free hand. "I, the Count Holman de Devonshire, being of sound mind, do hereby
relinquish all rights to the Castle Loma to my beloved
wife, the Contiesse Veronica Rosemead de Devonshire...."

There was no time to read more. With tears streaming down her face, Veronica ran down the dark hall
where water was now standing ankle-deep from the
gaping hole left when the one tower had toppled.
Signaling for Dr. Gillian and her mother to go ahead,
she climbed in the car. Brutus leaped into the seat
beside her. And, with Hilda and James following, the
three automobiles began the dark, slippery descent
of Enchanted Hill.

The ship's bells gave one last wild clang and then were silenced by an explosion such as Veronica had never heard before. The very road in front of her little car seemed to tremble with fear. Then the road bent sharply and the windshield wipers cleared space enough for her eyes to catch the nightmarish sight of a mighty wave rolling back to sea. Taking with it sections of turrets and towers. Precious pieces that could never be replaced. And, with them, family secrets. All for burying at sea. The seawall had given way. . . .

• • •

Veronica shivered as she entered the door at the doctor's house even though the air was heavy with the hot, humid breath of the storm. Her scarf had blown off and her hair clung to her face in dripping confusion. Every thread of her clothing was drenched by the rain against which no coat was a shield. But she must see Rhoda and her brother. Make sure they were all right. And ask more of her husband. His being alive was no longer enough.

"Where—?" But Dr. Gillian was pointing to a closed door even before she could finish the question.

The face, swathed in bandages, was unrecognizable in the shadow-filled room. "Gilbert—" Rushing to his bedside, she knelt to take his hand.

"The name, my dear contiesse is—"

But Veronica heard no more. Holman! "You look terrible," she whispered, the unreality of it all not penetrating fully.

The strange eyes appraised her in the familiar, teasing manner. "And you, my dear, look beautiful."

"You can't see. You have a concussion!" Futilely,

she pushed at her dripping hair, dropping his hand. Then faltering, she whispered, "You let me think you were dead. You—you made no effort to get in touch—let me know—"

"There was no need." His voice sounded remote. "You should have your chance for happiness with Thurman. He's finished with his assignment."

"And gone," she added softly.

For a moment her husband seemed to hesitate. But there was no hesitancy in his next words. "You have what you wanted. Your precious Castle Loma."

Veronica could not bring herself to fight. "It is gone—most of it—and, anyway, it belonged to you no matter what your later decision was."

There was a long silence. Veronica wondered if she had reached him. How does a woman make a man see that she loves him? Not for his key to power. That had been a key to conflict, too. Not for what she learned his true purpose to be. But because of love itself—love for whatever he had been, was, or ever would be. . . .

It was the old, debonair Holman Devonshire who broke the silence. "Are you aware that I came here with an ulterior motive?"

She nodded.

"Then you know why it was necessary to play the part I played. Perhaps too well at times, but that is my style. Maybe it will explain the collection of acquaintances." He paused, then shrugging as if it didn't matter whether Veronica understood, said flatly, "My job is finished here. I will be leaving."

Veronica's heart was breaking. "On another assignment?" *Oh, take me with you, Holman! One man wants me to accompany him. I refuse. I offer myself to another. And he rejects me.*

It didn't matter, she thought tiredly. It was impossible from the start. There was Mother. And her brother. Where they would go or what they could do was more than her mind could cope with. But they were not this man's problems.

Realizing that she was still kneeling, Veronica rose stiffly to her feet and stared unseeingly at the puddle of water her wet clothing had left on the faded carpet. Murmuring that she must change, Veronica was about to leave the room when Holman spoke.

"I won't be going on another assignment," he said matter-of-factly in response to her unanswered question. "This was to have been my last one anyway. And when the news breaks, I will be of no further use as an undercover man. Of course, that leaves the underworld characters who may be seeking me out." He laughed without much mirth. "That's good. A man needs excitement in his life. I can never ignore a challenge!"

And who wants to be tied to a wife? Particularly a clumsy frump. . . .

She turned away before he could see the pain in her eyes.

• • •

The next few days were busy. And revealing. Her mother made no mention of Castle Loma and, at Dr. Gillian's advice, Veronica did not pressure her to use her legs. It would all take time. Gilbert, very subdued, was waited on hand and foot by a dewy-eyed Rhoda. The girl had achieved what none of the others had been able to—added enough starch to Gil's backbone to get him to give himself up. Dr. Gillian had spoken with the district attorney's office who would be willing

to go along with partial restitution for the money he
had collected for counterfeit sales. Of course, the DA's
job was to represent the people, but given a good attorney,
the boy might get off with a light sentence. Not that he
could promise.

"And I'll wait!" Rhoda said with a radiant smile.
Why not what with the two of them getting married?
Yes, *married*—to think that such a man would marry
the likes of her, a cocktail waitress. . . .

"Well, it just might work out at that," the doctor
told Veronica, who had been too astonished to comment. "The reverend says the Lord has strange ways,
which we all know. Says, too, he's never paired off
a couple and have the marriage fail." He looked at
her quizzically. Veronica felt her face color and turned
away.

She stayed away from Holman, feeling that was
what he would want. Dr. Gillian was keeping a heavy
schedule and she knew he was exhausted. Hospitals
were filled, but he made house calls. Veronica volun-
teered her services as a nurse until the emergency
ended, mostly to get away from the house where her
husband lay out of danger but not yet ready to move
on.

Hurricane Mario had lowered its voice and, lifting
its skirts of rain, moved inland. The gigantic task
of cleaning up was underway. Veronica longed for the
time when she could drive up to check on the full extent
of damage to Castle Loma. Probably nothing remained.

When at last the day arrived, she spoke with Dr.
Gillian about leaving Mother in his care. For answer
the kindly man gave her a look of amusement.

At length he said, "Your mother and I have a perfect understanding, my child. I've known what you are
just finding out for years. And, as for the future, well—"
his eyes twinkled merrily as he wiped his glasses,

"let's just say that we talked about more than her health during those cribbage games! Maybe the reverend's right—"

"Oh, Dr. Gillian, I—I don't know what to say!" She rushed into his arms with a hug of genuine affection.

"Say nothing at all," he said gently. "Just get on with your life—beginning with a jaunt up Enchanted Hill."

The damage was no more and no less than Veronica had expected. Castle Loma appeared beyond repair. At least, the part that had made it into a "castle." Nothing stood except the tower encasing her father's beloved ship's bells. The downstairs wall stood in part, the windows staring like sightless eyes deprived of glasses.

Sadly, Veronica turned away. Maybe a few things remained in the rubble, but her heart was too heavy to search. She needed a moment with God. Hardly aware of her direction, she walked toward her Secret Garden, picking her way carefully along the crumbled walls and fallen trees. Nothing familiar was in her refuge. It was washed clean then layered with broken bricks. Idly picking up several of the shards to form a little bench, Veronica was surprised to be greeted by the distinct odor of mint. Digging deeper, as if it were important, she unearthed more and more of the little vine that refused to die. Gratefully, she picked a handful of the peppermint, crushed the leaves and inhaled deeply. Silently, then aloud, she prayed.

For a moment, she thought it was only her imagination that warned of another presence. Burying her face more deeply into the bruised mint, she continued her low prayer of thanksgiving—"and safety of those I love." She must ask forgiveness for being judgmental. . . .

When she paused, a deep, resonance broke the silence. "You must be Miss Rosemead? Then allow me to introduce myself—"

Holman! And repeating almost verbatim his words

of their first meeting. *How different everything might have been—*

But her thought went unfinished. Holman exploded into a violent sneeze. A laugh Veronica hadn't known was coming rippled up inside her and burst in the late-afternoon air.

"Do that again, Veronica!" Even above the nasal twang of his voice, she sensed a strong emotion. "You don't know how good it sounds to hear you laugh."

"You don't know how good it feels," she answered honestly, letting herself laugh again at his second sneeze.

"And now, my dear, if you will please step out of that stinking mint bed—"

Veronica dropped the mint leaves, wiped her hands on her skirt and wiped away the traces of a smile. There was nothing to laugh about between the two of them.

"I suppose," Holman said as they reached safer ground, "that I am indebted to that pesky stuff! It led me to you and I want to show you something before I go."

"Go?"

Looking at him for the first time, Veronica saw that the heavy bandages were gone leaving only angry scars which were even more extensive than she had realized. He could have been killed!

Involuntarily, she gave a little cry. But he waved away all concern. "I've survived worse in my line of work."

She realized then that they were back to the ruins of her childhood home. Holman was pointing toward the back. "The basement's still intact—and locked."

At her questioning glance, he explained as if it were important, "Your heirlooms are there. When I saw what your brother was up to I stashed them away. Here's hoping the whole episode and Rhoda's steadying influence will save his young neck—are you crying? About *him*?"

"About everything," Veronica was unable to keep the words from tumbling out, "you—me—Mother—Gil—life—"

Her husband reached out his arms. "Don't cry, Veronica," he whispered huskily. "It will all work out for you. Just think of what lies ahead—what you will do now," he murmured against her hair.

"Try to patch up my life—"

"And your heart? Oh, Veronica, why must you always try to mend things before seeing if they will work?"

"Because," she said, blowing her nose on the handkerchief he gave her, "Because it was all an act—everything you did—even our marriage—" She burst into tears again.

Holman returned the handkerchief. "Not *all* an act. My marriage was premeditated. I was in the village before you knew—watching you—wishing my life were different." He spoke the next words slowly as if unable to believe them himself. "The part about the priesthood was real, too. I almost entered the Lord's service, you know."

"You mean—"

"I mean," Holman spaced each word, "that I used to think man shapes his own destiny—that I could shape events—"

Veronica had stopped crying. In the loose circle of his arms, she held her breath. "And now?" she whispered.

"And now I know differently. You and God have shown me that events shape man. I'd like to build a mission for homeless persons like Rhoda. She'll need help even now until Gilbert's release and then," he sighed, "he will, too. Bless his pin-head!" Excitement sharpened his voice.

The Castle Loma! A perfect spot. Enough could be built back. . . with means such as Holman had. . . and that would fulfill the promise to Rhoda. . . .

"I'll give you a divorce," she said woodenly, "so you can return to the priesthood."

There was a sharp intake of breath. "I don't need a divorce to run a mission! I need a wife—"

"Then stay Holman—*please* stay! All my life I've made promises to people...my father...my mother...you. Please...at last, I want to make a promise that will last forever. A promise with *all* my heart." The words were torn from her throat.

His arms tightened. It was hard to breathe against the steel band of his muscles. And, for the first time, Veronica heard him fumble for words. "You mean—you can't mean you want to be my wife—a real wife—in every sense of the word? I warned you that an invitation—you *mean*—?"

Veronica struggled just enough to look into the strange eyes, lovelit to match in color. "Yes," she said demurely, "Your Royal Highness, I do!—"

With all my heart....